HOPE FOR CHRISTMAS

RACHELLE J. CHRISTENSEN

Praise for

***Rachelle J. Christensen's
Echo Ridge Romance Series***

Hope for Christmas

"This sweet romance is the perfect holiday read and will make you believe in the power of love and happily ever after."

—Cindy Roland Anderson, author of *Under a Georgia Moon*

The Princess Bride of Riodan

"I disappeared into this book and the sweet town of Echo Ridge for the evening. Can't wait to go back!"

—Lucy McConnell, author of the *Dating Mr. Baseball* series

Coming Home to Love

"Rachelle Christensen creates a town we'd all like to live in and people we'd all like to be friends with."

—Janette Rallison, author of *How I Met Your Brother*

✺ Created with Vellum

Get your free book!

CHAPTER 1

THE SILVER BELL CHIMED AS ANIKA FLETCHER entered Kenworth's department store. She took two steps forward then stopped when she saw a glint of metal. Crouching, she picked up the quarter next to the toe of her worn black boot. She stamped the last bit of snow from her heels and pocketed the quarter. With only fifty dollars left until the next paycheck, Anika needed every last cent.

"Whatcha got, Mommy?" Four-year-old Megan scrunched her nose and lifted up on her tiptoes.

Anika smiled at her daughter and touched the end of her little pixie nose. "Just a coin."

"We need lots of money so we can pay Beatrice." Megan's voice held no trace of concern.

Anika frowned. Thank goodness her daughter was so

even-tempered. The daycare manager, Beatrice, had turned them away fifteen minutes ago.

"I'm sorry dear, I really am. Megan is such a sweetheart but we can't let her stay until you pay your bill. You still owe one-hundred and thirty dollars." Beatrice had given her a look filled with pity before slowly closing the door.

Anika's face heated recalling the humiliating conversation. She felt Megan's tiny fingers wrapping around her hand, and looked down. Megan was like her anchor in the stormy seas. Anika blinked twice, rolled her shoulders back, and smiled at Megan. "It's going to be okay."

She adjusted her name tag and walked past the fragrance counter holding her breath, even inhaling the rich scents seemed too expensive for someone like her. This was a seasonal job, but Anika wanted to work into a full-time position.

They walked past The Candy Counter with its rows and rows of hand-dipped chocolates that made Anika's stomach grumble. She'd skipped lunch, saving the last three slices of bread for Megan. The peanut butter and jelly sandwich she'd made for their dinner called to her from the sack inside her purse.

"Can I have a candy, Mommy?" Megan tugged on Anika's hand.

"Not now. Mommy has to go to work."

Two boys stood next to the display, pointing at the

neat row of mint patties. "These are Mom's favorite. Let's get them for Christmas."

The older brother, who looked to be about ten or eleven pointed at the prices. "Tommy, see how much it is a pound? I don't think we have enough." He studied a handful of coins, his lips moving as he counted. "We need seventeen more cents. We could get some of the taffies instead."

"But Mom loves those." Tommy stuck his finger on the glass in front of the mint patties.

Anika hesitated, watching the boys recount their money. She looked over at her daughter and remembered how last week Megan had begged to give a quarter to the Salvation Army bell ringer outside Kenworth's. Anika had clutched tightly to the coin before giving it to Megan. When had she become so hard and tight that she couldn't even let go of a quarter? What hurt more was watching another woman in a beautiful suede coat— likely one of the tourists everyone referred to as *Ice Money*— shush her child and drag him into the store, denying his same request.

She slid the quarter out of her pocket and took a step closer to the Candy Counter. "Here, this might help you boys. I bet your Mom would love those mint patties."

Tommy looked up and grinned, then glanced at his older brother who studied Anika and the quarter in her outstretched hand. Anika nodded and moved her hand a fraction of an inch closer. The coin wasn't enough to buy a treat for Megan, but maybe it could help the boys. The older boy took the quarter, adding it to his handful of change.

"Thank you." He grinned and both boys turned back to the counter.

Anika smiled, and lifted one shoulder in a half-shrug. She wasn't counting on the quarter anyway, and it was cute to see how excited the boys were. Megan tugged on Anika's other hand and she continued over to the women's department.

Usually Anika parked around back and entered near the offices and employee lounge, but she hadn't figured out what to do about Megan yet. She led her daughter to the checkout station in the women's department, happy that no one had noticed their arrival. Anika stowed the oversized bag full of Megan's toys under the counter and pulled out a few dolls. She cleared a space in the cabinet under the cash register for Megan to play. It was breaking the rules to bring a child to work, but Anika hoped that she could keep Megan quiet and entertained for the next four hours. She was only scheduled to work part-time for the holidays, mostly covering a half-shift. She tried not to think about what she would do next week when she was scheduled for six-hour shifts.

Thankfully Kenworth's wasn't overly busy for a Tuesday, even if it was December first and the Christmas countdown was officially on. The mad rush yesterday on Santa's first day had spiked the store's attendance, but things were slowing down a bit and the man in the red suit had left his throne for a break. Anika shushed Megan each time a customer approached and did her best to keep up with her duties in the women's department.

Megan munched on her peanut butter sandwich, looked at books, and played with her toys, but by eight o'clock she was tired and Anika had run out of ideas.

"I want gummies!" Megan stamped her foot and cried.

"Shh, Meg. We have to be very quiet so we don't scare the shoppers," Anika infused a soothing tone into her voice, but it wasn't very convincing. Her own stomach tightened, grumbling with the gnawing hunger that she'd grown accustomed to. A pack of gummies, or any food right at the moment would be welcome. Anika picked Megan up and rocked her back and forth, humming along to the tune of *Silent Night* playing over the sound system.

Anika saw her boss round the corner and wished she could climb under one of the racks of designer clothes she'd just arranged. The woman had steel gray hair, a temper that matched it, and eyebrows that were perpetually arched in a slant of disgust with everyone and everything she came in contact with.

Cecilia Grange, acting CEO of Kenworth's Department store walked toward Anika and pointed her long finger at Megan. "I take it this is your daughter?"

"Yes, I apologize," Anika's voice was just above a whisper. "I didn't have another option tonight."

"Was she the one I just heard crying? We don't want to annoy our patrons." Cecilia's strident tone made it clear who was annoyed.

"I'm really sorry. I've got her settled down now." Anika turned so that Cecilia could see Megan's angelic face. Her daughter smiled at Cecilia just as Anika had hoped. She saw her boss soften a fraction.

Cecilia's eyebrow lowered a millimeter. "Well, as long as she's quiet, I guess we can make an exception."

Anika didn't promise that it would never happen again because she still hadn't figured out what to do with Megan tomorrow during her shift. "Thank you. She's really a good little girl and won't cause any trouble."

Cecilia pursed her lips. "I came to talk to you about the overtime you signed up for. Are you still capable of filling it?"

"Yes, I'd be glad to help however I can." Anika tried to tone down the desperate eagerness she heard in her voice.

"We're setting up a giving tree," Cecilia said. "It's one of Keira's projects." She rolled her eyes and huffed as though Keira's ideas were only meant to torture her. "I'm going along with it because I have to humor some people. After the store closes tonight I need you to set up the tree."

Anika swallowed hard and nodded. "I can certainly do that."

"Then you'll need to decorate it and help with the handmade cards we're creating to hang on the tree. We have an association that will be supplying names of those in need this holiday season." Cecilia pointed at a long box on the other side of the counter. "The tree is in there. We want it completed by tomorrow night."

"I can do that." Anika shifted Megan in her arms. Thankfully, her daughter remained quiet, probably scared silent by Cecilia's eyebrows.

Cecilia glanced at Megan and back at Anika. "Good."

After the tapping of her heels faded, Anika looked at the box holding the Christmas tree and groaned. Anika's stomach grumbled, protesting the lack of food. It was going to be a long night.

"MEGAN, honey, move your dolls and car back behind the counter." Anika pointed at the toys she'd nearly tripped over on her way to unbox the Christmas tree.

"Okay, Mommy, in a minute," Megan answered, and then continued talking to her dolls.

It was nine o'clock and Kenworth's was officially closed. Anika was tired but she still had to straighten the changing rooms and count out her till. Megan should've been in bed an hour ago, but since her little tantrum she'd been good-natured about playing in the cupboards and shelves behind the counter.

Anika stooped and ripped the packing tape off the box. The artificial tree burst from its confines like a Jack-in-the-box, startling her. She sucked in a breath and put a hand over her heart. There were dozens of branches with color-tipped ends. She couldn't see the trunk though it must be in there somewhere. The tree was squished and flat. It would take a degree in engineering to figure this thing out.

"Stupid Christmas tree," she muttered. If it weren't for Megan, she'd skip Christmas altogether. The holiday was a slap in the face to someone like Anika— a divorced, single mom with a deadbeat ex. She hadn't been able to locate Jimmy after he'd been released from jail the last time, but she was tired of hiding from him. When she moved to Echo Ridge a year ago, she decided a fresh start would be the best solution to her problems. The sleepy little New York town had been full of promises and hope, but after losing her job two months ago when Megan was hospitalized with pneumonia, everything had changed. Although the state had helped pay for Megan's treatment, Anika had fallen farther and farther behind.

Her chest tightened when she thought about what was around the next corner. This job was temporary, and Anika had run out of options. If she didn't find something soon, she'd be evicted from her one bedroom apartment.

She pulled the tree trunk upright and began putting together the sections of the tree. It took much longer than it should have with bits of the white flock crumbling and sticking to her clothes. One of the branches refused to straighten, the end was all twisted and it took her nearly ten minutes to smooth out the kinks. Anika grumbled to herself about the fake tree and its apparent mission to annoy her by not snapping together correctly. She fiddled with the pre-lit strands that had to be connected in several places. There were three different cords to test the lights, but she couldn't get them all to work together. The box said the lights were supposed to twinkle, but Anika couldn't even get more than one strand to turn on at a time. She grumbled and stepped back— on Megan's dolls. Anika's foot turned, she gasped, and fell forward into the tree with a shriek.

Before she could react to the fake evergreen needles poking her in the face, strong hands pulled her back from the mass of lights and cords.

"Are you hurt?"

Anika blinked and looked up at the man who had spoken. Her mouth opened and closed, and she shook her head. If Enrique Iglesias had come to her rescue then she was definitely going to thank the blasted Christmas tree. She rubbed a hand over her face and saw that he wasn't Enrique, but with the shadow of scruff along his chin and his slightly mussed black hair against caramel skin, he could be Enrique's younger brother. Anika shook her head. She was gawking, and hadn't answered his question. "I'm not sure," she said.

"Let's get you away from this tree. I don't think it likes you." He cupped his hand under her forearm, carefully lifting her off the ground.

Anika winced when she put weight on her foot. "Ouch. I kind of twisted my ankle."

"Sit down right here and I can take a look at it." His dark hair matched his chocolate brown eyes and Anika found herself wondering again if Enrique did have a younger brother.

He helped her sit, leaning next to the wood paneling of her checkout station. He crouched down and held out his hand. "I'm Carlos Rodriguez. I'm a volunteer fireman, so I have some medical training. Mind if I take a look?" He had a Spanish accent, not heavy, but alluring, and Anika listened to him appreciatively.

"Oh, it's just my ankle. I'm sure it'll be fine in a few minutes." Anika winced again when she moved her toes. "My name's Anika Fletcher." She held out her hand and Carlos shook it, his grip firm, yet gentle at the same time. Anika tore her eyes away from him and reached down to examine her ankle. It didn't appear to be swelling, but every tendon around the bone ached. Maybe she should have him look at it. "Ugh, this is just what I didn't need tonight." She leaned over and massaged the tender side of her ankle. It wouldn't cost her anything to have him look at it. "Okay, maybe I'd better have you look." She moved back so that Carlos could see her ankle.

He leaned over and gently pulled her pant leg up. His fingers were warm, and he pressed lightly around her ankle. Anika's heart sped up— it was hard to ignore the flutter in her stomach as he carefully examined her foot. He looked over at her and smiled. "There might be a little swelling later, but it's a good sign that it's not turning colors. You need to ice it and wrap it to stabilize the area."

Anika let out the breath she'd been holding when he released her foot. "Okay, thanks for your help. I was trying to get that dang tree figured out. It definitely doesn't like me and the feeling is mutual."

Carlos walked over to the tree, now standing almost ten feet tall, and shifted a few branches. Then he crouched down by the electrical outlet. "You know, this could be considered a fire hazard."

Anika straightened and leaned forward to look at the surge protector. Had she plugged in too many cords? She scrunched her nose counting the four cords snaking from the tree to the power source. "I didn't think that was too many." She looked over at him.

Carlos grinned. He was teasing her! And his smile made those dark eyes light up— the ones that were looking at her with appreciation.

Anika smiled, started to lean forward, but then she

pulled back abruptly. "Thanks for your help. I'd better get back to work." She gave her head a little shake, reminding herself that *all* men were off limits no matter how closely they were related to Enrique Iglesias.

"The store's closed. Aren't you about finished?" Carlos glanced around the empty department store.

Anika followed his gaze to the flickering light above the toys and strollers in the back of the store. Beyond that light in the back offices, Cecilia was probably still hard at work, and Anika couldn't afford to be caught sitting around. "Yes, I'm just putting in some overtime to get this tree set up."

Carlos crouched next to the tree and fiddled with the cords. "This must be new. I don't remember seeing a tree set up in this department last year." When Anika gave him a curious look, he explained. "I've done a lot of the remodeling in this store over the past few years." Carlos thumbed behind him. "I'm finishing up some shelves over in the children's section this week."

"Oh, I noticed those. They look really nice," Anika said. She forced herself to turn her gaze from Carlos's muscular shoulders to the remodeling of the children's section. There were three rows of new shelves against the wall, the light oak wood spanning a length of about five feet. She could imagine how nice it would be to display different items.

"Thanks," Carlos's voice was muffled. "Now, let's see if that works."

He flipped the switch and the tree lit up with twinkling white lights.

"You fixed it," Anika said. She hopped closer to the tree and touched one of the white lights. "Thank you."

Carlos chuckled. "Glad I could help." He straightened the tree and turned to Anika. "How's your ankle?"

"It's a little tender, but I think it will be fine." Anika held herself carefully so as not to put too much weight on her foot. Her curiosity motor was spinning rapidly over the fireman who'd just saved her and the Christmas tree. The way he stood there with that bit of coarse stubble lining his jaw made her want to reach out and touch it. No, wait. She clenched her hands into fists. She most certainly did not want to touch him, or any man for that matter.

This was Kenworth's and she was an employee, she needed to focus. She wiped her hand over her mouth, straightened her shoulders and said, "Thanks again for your help. I'd better finish up now."

"How much work do you have left tonight? I'll probably be here for another hour." Carlos smiled at her and she could almost see the wheels in his mind turning. He looked like he was on the verge of asking her out. She didn't have time for this.

"Well, I'm hoping to be finished soon because my daughter—" Anika stopped talking and turned toward the cash register. "Megan!" She hadn't heard a sound from her daughter for the past several minutes while she was caught up ogling forbidden territory.

Anika scrambled around the counter. Megan wasn't there. She looked up and met Carlos's gaze, his eyes searched hers, and she could see her panic mirrored there for an instant.

"Your daughter?" he came around the corner and scanned the floor littered with Megan's toys.

"She was right here playing. She's four, with brown hair and blue eyes— looks just like me. I'll check the break room." Anika moved to pass Carlos, but he stopped her, putting a hand on her arm.

"Wait, what's that?" he pointed to the corner of a pink and white polka-dotted blanket hanging out of the cupboard under the register—Megan's blanket.

Anika's breath caught in her throat and her heart double-timed, pounding against her rib cage. She crouched and opened the cupboard. The breath whooshed out of her when she saw Megan curled up with her blanket, sleeping in the cramped space among rolls of receipt paper, sacks, and cloth shopping bags. Anika sat back on the floor and squeezed her eyes shut. "Thank goodness."

She felt a hand on her back and looked over to see Carlos crouching next to her. "She's cute. That's quite a hiding place."

"My word, that scared me to death. I'm so glad you

saw her blanket. Thank you." Anika moved to stand, but her ankle didn't cooperate and she stumbled into Carlos.

His arms moved around her, quickly righting her and then letting her go. "Do you need help getting her to your car? I don't mind carrying her."

Anika opened her mouth to say no, but with her ankle she'd have to accept his help. Her mind was still a few seconds behind, feeling the strength of his arms as he caught her, the solid muscles of his body holding her upright. *Focus, Anika!* She glanced at the clock. It was already past ten, she was exhausted. "I guess I'll finish the tree tomorrow night. Are you sure you don't mind carrying her?"

Carlos grinned. "Not at all. A fireman is trained to complete his rescues."

"Well, you've saved me twice tonight," Anika replied. She was gushing, and thanking this guy way too much. He was just being polite. She needed to get a grip and quit smiling at him. But every time she smiled, he would smile back and it made her stomach do a little flip that she was sure meant trouble.

"It's my pleasure. Do you think she'll wake up when I lift her?" he crouched next to Megan's sleeping form.

"I would be very surprised. She sleeps like a rock. Her name's Megan." Anika said. "Let me just grab my things here."

"You might want to turn off the tree for the night.

Cecilia warned me not to overload the circuits. I guess the electrical wiring in this building is pretty old."

Anika nodded and flipped off the lights. She watched as Carlos gently knelt next to her daughter and lifted Megan into his arms. The child sighed and pulled her blanket tighter. Carlos held her tenderly and smiled, lifting his eyes to meet Anika's. The way he held her so carefully did something dangerous to Anika's heart. It was like the moment a match slides across the side of the box igniting an explosion of heat that pops and sizzles. And she couldn't afford to play with fire.

CARLOS NOTICED THE WAY ANIKA'S throat tightened and then relaxed when he lifted Megan from the cupboard. She kept a close eye on him, as if she wasn't sure whether to trust him or not. Her blue eyes were full of stories. Stories he would have liked to hear, if she'd let him. Something about the tightness around her eyes and the stiffness in her movements told him she was on guard. There were snippets of interest in her glance and it was enough to give him the encouragement to hang around.

She pointed. "I'm right out front today."

He nodded and followed her out to the beat up Nissan Sentra with a crappy red paint job and no hubcaps. She hurried to unlock the door, still favoring her ankle, and moved a few items out of the way. She stood by the door of the car and smiled at him as he moved to place Megan in the car. He hesitated for a second, meeting Anika's gaze. She was stunning in the soft glow of the street light with a few strands of her light brown hair curling softly around the nape of her neck where it had escaped the bun. He wondered how long her hair was, and if it was as soft as it looked. Carlos had noticed her earlier from across the store and wondered if he should try to strike up a conversation. Lucky for him, the Christmas tree had provided the perfect introduction.

He tucked Megan into the car and buckled her seat-belt. "You're right. She is a heavy sleeper." He stepped back from the car, closing the door quietly. He lifted his eyes to Anika's and nodded.

She adjusted the straps on her bag. "Well, I'd better get her home. Thanks so much for your help."

He didn't want her to leave. He wanted to stand there for a few more minutes and talk, but it would have to wait. Anika moved to open her car door, but Carlos opened it for her. The way she stood so straight made her appear tall, but when she ducked into her car, Carlos guessed she was about five foot six. "Maybe I'll see you tomorrow night."

Anika hesitated, and then gave him a tentative smile. "Maybe."

Carlos rubbed a hand along the back of his neck as she pulled out of the parking lot. The evening was cold with clouds threatening snow. He shivered as her tail lights disappeared around the corner. Tomorrow he'd come in a bit earlier to get started and see if there might be another opportunity to chat with Anika.

He hurried back inside to clean up his tools and get ready for his next eight hours on call in the Echo Ridge Volunteer Fire Department. The town was small so they operated on a tight budget which meant that all of the firemen had other jobs. For Carlos, it kept him busy, sometimes too busy because he hadn't been on a date for two months. His madre had pestered him last time they talked, "Twenty-seven is too old to be single. You should be giving me grandbabies by now." He smiled thinking of her rapid Spanish and the thick accent that accompanied her words when she spoke in English.

Five years ago his mother had moved from Puerto Rico to sunny Florida. She didn't understand why her son wanted to live in a cold climate such as upstate New York. But Carlos loved Echo Ridge, the town was small enough that he waved at several people on his way to work each day, but big enough that he'd been able to keep his own business afloat. The smog steered clear of Echo Ridge and the buildings had character, with old-style architecture that would continue to be in need of his carpentry skills. Even though people seemed busier than they used to, he liked the slower pace compared to some of the bigger cities he'd visited.

With his tools tucked safely inside the back of his

pickup, Carlos drove a mile east of the store, up a slight hill and pulled into the three-bedroom bungalow he called home. The front porch leaned to one side, but new shingles covered several parts of the roof. He hadn't started replacing the windows yet, which were all aluminum frames, but the new front door was locked and secure. He'd purchased the home last year just before foreclosure. Every paycheck he bought more supplies to fix up the place and it was looking better, but wasn't anything to be proud of yet. Who was he kidding? There was a reason he wasn't married. Who would want a college dropout who lived in a rundown house, even if it was close to Parley's Way and its posh residents?

Carlos had picked up a few good clients from the Ice Money population that flocked to Echo Ridge during ski season but it wasn't steady enough to support a family yet. He thought of the woman he'd met tonight. She had a daughter and would need someone stable. Carlos pursed his lips. Maybe it'd be better if he didn't bump into her at the store. He pulled open the new kitchen cabinets he'd installed last summer— the white paint gleaming under the recessed can lights above the sink. Maybe he should take his mother's advice and sell this place for a profit, move closer to family, and the sunshine of Miami. He shook his head, halting the negative train of thoughts. The desire to fix up the place still burned inside, and he couldn't ignore the visions he had of the newly remodeled home, perfect for a little family. It might not be his family, but he would keep working until he finished this place. He had that much time at least to make up his mind about his future in Echo Ridge.

ANIKA FOLDED A STACK OF SHIMMERY sweaters for the holiday display next to her cash register. Kenworth's had been busy when she first came in at five o'clock, but the Wednesday night crowd was thinning out. A good thing because Megan was growing tired of playing on the floor. She had visited Santa earlier and told him in great detail about the dollhouse she wanted. The hollow place inside Anika ached when she heard the hope and joy in Megan's voice. The child had complete faith that Santa Claus would bring her exactly what she asked for.

Her daughter zoomed through the clothing racks with a Care Bear under her arm— the toy Anika had found at a yard sale last summer for a dollar. Too bad there weren't any yard sales in December.

Only two more days until pay day, maybe she'd have

enough to buy Megan the gift she really wanted, but no. Anika chewed on her bottom lip. If she paid the daycare there definitely wouldn't be enough, and if she didn't pay them she'd have to keep bringing Megan to work with her. Anika pressed her fingers against the soft sweaters. There had to be another option. She was just too tired to see it right now.

Someone had come in earlier with a sheet of labels to put in the cards on the Hope Tree. Anika hadn't looked, but she knew they contained information about people in need, children mostly, with specific sizes and toy requests for people to purchase to make their Christmas wishes come true. She'd spent some time creasing the cards to hang on the tree, making sure each one contained a label that was adhered perfectly straight according to Cecilia's command. The cream-colored cards were edged to look like snowflakes and they hung from a golden string that reflected the overhead light. Silver and gold bells dangled from the branches and chimed softly whenever someone bumped up against the tree. Anika clenched her teeth. How ironic that it was her job to decorate the tree. Maybe the overtime would be enough to pull her out of the financial crevice she'd been stuck in for the past six years.

A woman walked by, trailing the scent of expensive perfume and toting a shopping bag overflowing with goods. That woman had no idea what a difference one-hundred dollars could make in someone's life. Anika swallowed, and breathed out her mouth so she wouldn't have to smell the fragrance of money she'd never have.

She arranged the sweaters carefully with a bit of gold tinsel snaking around the table. Megan zipped past, bumped into her elbow, tripped, and crashed into the pile of ornaments Anika was supposed to hang on the Christmas tree tonight. She heard the high note of breaking glass and sucked in a breath.

"Sorry, Mommy," Megan whimpered.

Anika snatched her from the floor, quickly scanning her daughter for any injuries, and then holding her firmly. "I want you to go sit on your blanket behind the cash register while I clean this up."

Megan's lips turned into a pout but Anika narrowed her eyes and shook her head. Her stomach clenched when she found the first broken ornament. It was a green and white glass ball, or it had been. Now shards of the thin glass littered the area. It was almost nine o'clock, hopefully there wouldn't be any customers coming in this late and she could get everything cleaned up.

She sorted through the rest of the boxes, and her heart returned to normal speed— there weren't any other broken ornaments. She picked up a large piece of the green glass and bent to throw it away. The clicking of heels behind her ratcheted her heart into her throat. She turned to see Cecilia round the corner and take in the situation.

Megan chose that moment to pop up from behind the counter and yell, "Boo!"

Cecilia jumped, glanced at Megan with distaste and turned to Anika. "If you want to keep your job, you need to be responsible for your daughter."

"Sorry." Anika pointed to her daughter. "Megan, sit down and be quiet. Now is not the time to play peek-a-boo."

"And what happened here?" Cecilia tapped her foot. Her frown lines deepened as she studied the bits of broken glass glistening from the polished wood floor.

"Megan tripped and broke an ornament. I'll get it cleaned up." Anika didn't offer to pay for the ornament, but she felt the expectation in the current of air snapping around Cecilia's head.

"I shouldn't even have to say this, but your daughter isn't an employee here and we're not a daycare center." Cecilia's voice crept up the scale a few notes. Anika heard the threat.

"I know, and I'm sorry. I couldn't find anyone to watch her." Anika looked at the floor, swallowed the tiny fragment of pride she had left and begged. "Please, I really need this job. I've got some medical bills that are due, and I didn't have another choice."

Cecilia sighed. "We've all got bills to pay. Now, I'm going to treat you like a professional and I expect the same from you. Take care of your daughter."

"Excuse me, but can I help?" It was Enrique's brother

with the sexy scruff lining his jaw. Anika studied the way his broad shoulders were set, his hands clenched as if he was angry. She stared, trying to think of his name. *Carlos.* She remembered him saying he wanted to see her again tonight. He'd rescued her from the Hope Tree and now he was interrupting Cecilia's tirade.

"Anika's daughter broke the decorations for the Christmas tree," Cecilia said, as if Megan had destroyed everything instead of just one ornament.

"I can pay for the damages. Is it just a couple ornaments?" He gave Cecilia a tentative smile.

Anika's eyes flitted from him to Cecilia, and she gave herself a mental shake. "It was one. I'll get this mess cleaned up and you can take it out of my paycheck."

"The store can cover it," Cecilia huffed. "Just make sure it doesn't happen again." She turned and took two steps, and inclined her head toward Megan. "And find a sitter for your daughter."

The main lights in the store switched off. Anika watched her boss disappear down the dim hallway past the employee lounge. She wished she could crawl into a dark hole and not come out until spring. Christmas would be over then and she wouldn't have to worry about this job, decorating trees, or buying presents.

"Hey, are you okay?" Carlos asked. "Don't let Cecilia get to you. She's grouchy to everyone. I can help you clean up."

Anika lifted her head. Carlos stood there with one

corner of his mouth turned up in a lopsided grin. He was incredibly handsome and there was something genuine about him and his concern for her that made her believe he was a decent guy.

She could see the tip of Megan's head behind him, and then her daughter's blue eyes peeked over the counter. Anika didn't have time to flirt with a guy; she didn't even have time for friends. Megan was her top priority and experience had taught her that most attractive, single guys weren't as interested in her daughter as they were about other things. A few months ago, Randy had treated her to a steak dinner and dessert, but then cornered her at his house asking for his "dessert".

She gritted her teeth and something snapped inside when she turned to Carlos. "I can take care of myself," Anika spat. "I don't need your charity."

"But I was just trying—" Carlos took one step back.

"You want to help?" Anika spun on her heel and ripped a tag off the tree. "There are plenty of people in this town you can help." She stuffed the card in his hand. "C'mon Megan." She hoisted her daughter on her hip and stomped past the tree toward the back of the store, putting as much space between her and Carlos as she could. She'd have to return in a few minutes to clean up the mess from the broken ornament. Her chest tightened. Gold tinsel, presents, ornaments, and people acting like Santa Claus. She hated Christmas.

CHAPTER 4

CARLOS BLINKED. WHAT HAD JUST HAPPENED? Apparently, Anika didn't want a knight in shining armor to save her or her Christmas tree. He nudged a piece of glass with his work boot. He looked up and saw the swish of Anika's ponytail, probably heading toward the employee break room. Something had happened to her. Carlos recognized the look he'd seen in her bright blue eyes. It wasn't right that a woman like her should hurt so much. Carlos figured that a man had probably been responsible for that hurt. He'd seen something like this once before, and many times in himself. Anika was pushing him away before he had the chance to get to know her. But she didn't know how determined he could be when someone gave him a challenge. He'd been about to give up on the possibility of Anika last night, but she'd just knocked him to the ground. She probably thought he didn't have a fighting chance. Carlos smiled and went to retrieve a broom.

He swept up the shards of glass and restacked a few boxes. When he heard someone approaching, he moved quickly back to the children's area to finish his work. The shelves lining the wall looked great. He just needed to polish them. The light oak was perfect against the dark hardwood floor. A cheerful braided rug in rainbow colors was centered among the boxes of books and toys. Carlos looked around Kenworth's and wondered if there was anything else he could do that would keep him in close proximity with Anika. The Kenworth building was nearly a hundred years old, and a person with an eye trained for renovation could see how much work had gone into keeping every geriatric feature in good repair. Someone had mentioned that the building had almost been demolished thirty years ago, but old man Kenworth was able to come up with enough funds to give the store a facelift and keep it going. Still, Carlos could see that much of the department store had a dated look, as if it was stuck in the 1980s.

The store was quiet and almost everyone had left, but he heard Anika speaking to her daughter occasionally. He took an armful of paper towels and his tool bucket out back. On his way in, he made a slight detour to see how Anika was coming along with her Christmas tree.

Carlos saw Megan sneak behind the counter and dart

into the cupboard under the register. Then she poked her head out and tickled Anika's leg.

"Hi Sweetie. I'm almost done and I'll be so glad. How about you?" Anika asked.

"I'll be so glad too, cuz Santa's coming," Megan replied.

Anika paused and clenched the ornament she was holding tightly in her hand. "Just remember that Santa has lots of kids to help this year so he's only bringing one thing to our house."

"I know and he's bringing me the best present ever!" Megan popped out of the cupboard, bouncing up and down. "A doll house for all my dollies. He'll bring it won't he, Mommy?"

Anika sighed. "Meg, honey, Santa is always watching out for us, for everyone, and he wants to do the right thing. Sometimes that means we don't get exactly what we ask for."

"But a doll house is the right thing," Megan said. She folded her arms and tucked herself back into the cupboard. "My dollies are tired. Can we go home now?"

"Soon."

"Are you going to decorate a tree for our house too?

"One tree is enough for me. You can look at this one all you want," Anika said as she hung the last few ornaments. Carlos moved toward the exit before she turned to see him eavesdropping. He carefully swept out the children's area, the entire time thinking about what

Megan had said. He missed his chance to help Anika to her car. She must have hurried out when he wasn't looking.

Carlos brushed his hands against his pants and pulled out the card Anika had shoved at him an hour ago. He studied the slightly crumpled card in his hand. **Girl, size 8, Jeans, shirt, pajamas.** A flicker of an idea ignited in his mind. He smoothed the card and folded it neatly into his wallet. There might be a way to help after all.

CHAPTER 5

ANIKA SLEPT LATE ON THURSDAY and took Megan to story time at the library. While Megan sat with the other children, she searched the internet for other job opportunities and babysitters, but she couldn't find anything in Echo Ridge. Her car was too old to handle a commute outside city limits, and with the winter weather, it wasn't a good idea for Megan's recovering lungs to be out and about. When she thought of the possibility of losing her job at Kenworth's her head throbbed and worry coursed through her veins. She hated feeling so close to the edge, like if she took one wrong step she'd tumble to the ground, pulling her unsuspecting child with her. Megan's trust in her mother was innocent and complete just as it was in Santa Claus, with no idea how fragile that trust felt to Anika. She knew that if they slipped, there would be nothing to break their fall.

The screen blurred before her eyes. She swiped a hand across her cheeks and straightened her shoulders. She would make this work. There had to be someone she could ask for help in tending Megan. The librarian with a German accent, Britta, had always been friendly toward her and Megan. Anika noticed Britta talking to a teenage girl with a blonde messy bun at the desk. The girl left the library carrying a stack of books. Maybe Britta could offer a recommendation for a teenager who might babysit Megan a few days a week. It had to be a cheaper option than daycare. She picked out a book and approached the circulation desk.

"Hey, Anika. It's so good to see you," Britta said. "How's Megan?"

"She loves story time. The puppets are her favorite." Anika set her book next to the scanner. "I'm looking for a babysitter for Megan, just during the holiday rush because I'm taking a few extra hours at Kenworth's. Do you know any teenage girls who could help me out?"

"My niece, Lila might be able to help you. I know she babysits for a few people in town," Britta said. "She was just in here. You might have seen her? She's seventeen, blonde hair in a bun."

Anika nodded. "I think I did see her. Could you help me get in touch with her?"

Britta smiled. "Sure. I bet she'd love your darling

Megan."

Ten minutes later, Anika left the library with Megan in tow and an armload of books. She actually smiled when someone wished her "Happy Holidays" because Lila would be babysitting Megan tonight. Her little girl would go to bed early for the first time in three days and Anika wouldn't have to worry about incurring Cecilia's wrath.

The thought of finishing up the Christmas tree didn't inspire happy Christmas melodies because Anika was sick of poking her arms into the fake needles. The ten-foot tree was mostly done, it was just taking longer than she'd expected to hang the dozens of cards in a way that made it easy for people to read the information each one contained. Even though she didn't like it, completing the job meant the end of the meager overtime work.

Anika involuntarily scanned the children's department every few minutes, looking for Carlos that evening but he must have finished up his project. She groaned. He was a nice guy and she'd been so rude to him. What was her problem? Her stomach growled in answer to her internal question. She was down to twenty-five dollars so she'd only brought an apple and a granola bar to work tonight. Lila would get at least half of that for babysitting. Thank goodness tomorrow was pay day. She caught herself looking for Carlos again and gave herself a mental slap. She had done the right thing scaring him off. She didn't need one more problem to deal with right now.

Anika wandered across the store to put away a few holiday items that were displayed near The Candy Counter. She waved at Reese Gates, the young woman who seemed to always be working behind the counter. Rumor on the sales floor was that Reese's grandma, a woman Anika had never met, had problems with dementia. Reese appeared to be close to Anika's age, single, and happy. Who wouldn't be when they worked every day surrounded by chocolate and had the security of a family business behind them?

"Hey, Anika. I'm closing up for the night and I have a bag of no-sales. I thought you and your daughter might like a few." Reese handed her a white sack that smelled heavenly.

"No-sales?" Anika asked.

"They aren't pretty enough to put in the display case but they still taste the same."

Anika clenched her stomach when it grumbled again and smiled at Reese. "That is so sweet. Thanks for thinking of us, but I don't want to take your chocolates."

"I'll have to throw them away if you don't and wouldn't Megan like them? There's a couple chocolate Santas in here that a box fell on." Reese shook the sack.

The smell of chocolate tickled Anika's nose. "Okay, then, if you're sure you can't use them."

"I'm sure." Reese handed her the bag.

"Thank you." Anika clenched her fingers and the white paper bag crinkled. "These smell so good."

"And taste even better." Reese smiled as she went back to filling the Turkish delight tray. The powdered sugar stuck to her gloves and found its way to her apron. "Where's Megan?"

"I actually found a babysitter for tonight so hopefully she's asleep in her own bed."

Reese nodded. "It looks like Carlos finished up those shelves." She looked past Anika toward the children's department. Anika turned to follow her gaze across the tiled walkway, but she couldn't see the shelves from this vantage point.

"He must have. What do you know about him?" Anika asked and then wished she hadn't.

Reese grinned. "Besides that finely sculpted chest I can imagine underneath his T-shirt?"

The image of Carlos's physique immediately came to mind and Anika blushed.

Reese giggled. "I noticed him checking you out yesterday."

"You did not," Anika said.

"I did." Reese nodded. "I was organizing some stuff in the store room. I guess I just blend in to the scenery around here because people don't notice me. I'd say Carlos might have a thing for you."

Anika felt her cheeks heat up a few more degrees. "That's probably not a good thing. I have a little girl and I'm not looking to complicate my life right now."

"Oh, trust me. I don't think anyone would call Carlos

a complication." Reese leaned against the counter and lowered her voice. "I don't know him real well, but my impression is that he's a quiet guy who works really hard, doesn't date much, and has turned down several of the um, empty-headed gals who fell all over themselves trying to catch his eye."

Anika listened, and tried to bite her tongue to keep from asking more questions about Carlos. Reese was nice but Anika didn't want to encourage any holiday matchmaking. "Well, that's good to know. I guess every once in a while someone attracts the right guy, but I'll steer clear of him, cuz that someone isn't me."

Reese studied her for a moment, her smile faltered. "I'm sorry to hear that. Don't worry. I think Carlos is on the shy side so he probably won't bother you if you don't want him to."

"Do you *want* him to bother *you?*" Anika asked. Dang, why couldn't she cut this conversation short?

"Well, I'm not really one to fight over a guy." Reese brushed away a piece of hair that had come loose from her long braid and left behind a streak of powdered sugar. "I want him to fight for me, so I don't think I need to worry about Carlos." She winked and headed back to the store room.

Anika thought about calling after her to tell her about the powdered sugar on her cheek, or that she wasn't interested in Carlos at all. Instead, she clamped her mouth shut and went back to work.

FRIDAY MORNING, CARLOS MET CECILIA at Kenworth's thirty minutes before the store opened to finalize his work and get paid for the shelves he'd built and installed. It was December fourth and he had finished the project one day ahead of schedule. People weren't big on remodeling this time of year so he had to make sure that the money from this job could last him into January. Part of him hoped that Cecilia might tip him for his excellent work and early timing, but his more realistic side shoved that thought out of his head as quickly as it had entered. If Cecilia's skin were green, she could pass as the Grinch's sister. He reminded himself to be extra nice to her anyway.

"Nice work, Carlos." Cecilia ran her hand over the shelves and rubbed her fingertips together as if she'd picked up a bit of imaginary dust.

Carlos had polished the shelving until it gleamed under the fluorescent lights last night, and he'd just wiped them down before she came to inspect the final project. "Thanks. I enjoy working here."

Cecilia's lips turned up a tiny bit at the corners, the closest she ever came to smiling. "It's very short notice but Keira and Tayton have come up with another plan to infuse *holiday magic* into the store." The way she spat the words *holiday magic* with so much distaste reminded Carlos again of his favorite Christmas cartoon featuring the Who with a heart two sizes too small. She drummed her red fingernails against the shelves. "They want to refurbish the old soda fountain."

"As in, get it up and running, dispensing soda and all?"

Cecilia rolled her eyes. "Yes, some nostalgic garbage that is a ridiculous waste of time. Tayton is getting the initial info on it. You'll need to be here at nine tomorrow morning to talk it over with Keira and Tayton— he's the new PR guy from the big city, come to save us all."

Carlos took her caustic comments in stride, filtering through the information she was offering him. "What kind of a timeline are they looking at? I'm guessing they want it done before Christmas."

"Yes, I think they mentioned something about having it done by the eighteenth."

Carlos couldn't keep his eyes from widening. "I'm a hard worker but that's going to be a tall order depending on how much renovation they want done."

"I agree," Cecilia said. "There may be one or two people around here that would like the extra hours. If you'd like, I can gather some names and give them to Keira."

Carlos hesitated. He usually worked alone, mostly because every extra dollar he earned he could put into fixing up his house. But two weeks to finish a project that he hadn't even started? He would need some help. "I'd like some suggestions. I'll talk to Keira."

"Good. Have a nice day." Cecilia handed him a gray business envelope and stalked off with her clipboard.

Carlos lifted the flap and glanced at the amount. It was what they had agreed upon, with no extras, but he was satisfied. Those dollars would help fund the bathroom remodel that he'd been putting off. And with the new project Cecilia had mentioned, he might be able to finish the bathroom before the end of the year. He tucked the envelope into his back pocket and walked across the store. He waved at Reese at the Candy Counter and stood in front of the housewares section. The old soda fountain was still there but it had been converted to a video rental counter at one time and now was central to the display area in housewares combined with an outdated snack area for teens. There were hideous looking shelves lining the back counter and much of the blue and white checkerboard tile was chipped and cracked along the edge of the counter. He gnawed on the inside of his cheek, closing his eyes for a minute to envision what the soda fountain might have looked like fifty years ago. A line of bar stools would have sat snugly under the lip of the counter, probably covered in red Naugahyde. Dangling lightbulbs would illuminate the back wall where someone served up ice cream sodas. When he opened his eyes, the modernized display crushed his daydreams. Signs covered the old mirror that was scratched and discolored along the edges. It was obvious that the soda fountain had been downsized at one point because the counter looked like it had been sawed off on one side. He shook his head. It would be an interesting meeting in the morning. Hopefully he could handle the job, because if he did, he'd be working at Kenworth's again. That meant another chance to see Anika.

THE FRIDAY NIGHT shopping rush had the air buzzing in Kenworth's. Anika felt like she'd been running back and forth across the department store all night. She straightened a few of the cards and ornaments on the Hope Tree. A slow burn of resentment stoked the embers of despair in the pit of her stomach. Every one of the cards on the tree represented a person who needed something. A person who had someone watching out for them. Anika didn't have any guardian angels or fairy godmothers, no family to help her. She had long since stopped wishing or praying that anything in her life would ever turn out. Each day felt like walking along a tightrope that was slowly unraveling before her.

Anika straightened the sign on the wrought iron easel that stood next to the tree. It was printed in a flowing script with information about the Hope Tree and how customers could reach out to those in need and even offer suggestions of more names to add to the tree. The Ladies League and Echo Ridge Christmas Council would verify each person's needs so that Kenworth's efforts could be maximized to help more local residents this holiday.

At five minutes to nine, Cecilia showed up with a gray business envelope that Anika hoped contained enough to cover all of her expenses and keep her afloat through the holidays.

"Hello, Cecilia." Anika didn't waste time saying anything past hello. She'd learned the hard way what happened when someone tried to make small talk with the boss.

"Anika." She gave her a curt nod and stepped toward the Hope Tree. "It would have been nice to have it completed earlier, but at least it's on display now." Cecilia's brows looked like she'd used a Sharpie to draw them in place. They stood out in stark contrast to her otherwise pale face. With her gray hair and light features, the eyebrows were as harsh as her boss. She handed Anika the envelope. "Here's your paycheck. In the future, I expect you to complete assignments promptly."

"Thank you." It was all Anika could do to keep from snatching the envelope from Cecilia's bony fingers. "Uh, do you know if there are any other overtime opportunities?"

Cecilia sighed. "There may be another opportunity for a few extra hours. I don't know if they'd be overtime, and it's probably outside your skill level, but Keira and Tayton, the PR guy from New York, are working on some details."

"Could you add my name to the list of interested applicants, please?" Anika heard the eagerness in her voice as a vision of Megan playing with a new dollhouse popped into her head.

Cecilia paused, her eyes moving over the tree and the sweater display Anika had set up. "Okay, I'll give Keira your name and we'll see what she says."

After she left, Anika opened the envelope, her heart pounding. The amount was a bit less than she'd hoped— she was never very good at figuring out how much tax would be taken out. She stared at the numbers, willing them to multiply inside the little box printed on blue paper. There wouldn't be enough for a dollhouse. It was just enough to pay for all of this month's expenses and Megan's hospital bill. The medical bills were on a three year plan through Ruby Mountain Hospital, but even that pinched at Anika's budget like a wicked stepsister.

She still didn't have enough for the daycare bill, but there was room to give them twenty dollars. Over time, she would pay her bills. Her shoulders slumped. She walked slowly out to the parking lot and shuddered at the icy wind howling through the streets. At least Megan was home safe and snug in bed tonight, even if she was dreaming of a magical Christmas that would never come to pass. Anika pressed her lips together. She would find a way to make her little girl's holiday special, even if there was no hope for Christmas.

CHAPTER 7

CARLOS WORE DRESS PANTS and a button down shirt for the meeting with Keira Kenworth. Her father was ill and from the looks of things, Kenworth's was struggling without the old man. Keira had grown up in Echo Ridge and it was obvious her interest in the store was beyond money. She and the new PR guy, Tayton Wells, sat down with Carlos and went over the plans to remodel the soda fountain.

"We want to rejuvenate Kenworth's, bring a sense of community spirit back to Echo Ridge," Keira said. "We want to give people a reason to step off Main Street and enjoy our little plaza like they did when I was a kid."

"And we want the store to be in the black this Christmas," Tayton said. He handed Carlos a grid with a timeline to complete the project. "We have a couple of investors interested in helping us breathe some new life into this place, which is why we decided to renovate the soda fountain. We'll bring back the old-time feel and add a new feature to the store that will attract customers."

Carlos looked over the design sheets and timeline. He rubbed his hand over the bit of stubble on his jaw. "I'm probably going to need to hire some help. Is there room in your budget for that?"

Keira nodded. "Yes, and through some persuasion—" she glanced at Tayton. "Cecilia has agreed to have a few temps who could probably help with some of the cleanup if you'd like to use someone Kenworth's has already approved to work here." She handed him an index card with a list of four names.

Carlos took the card and felt a little jolt when he saw the first name on the list, Anika Fletcher. Someone or something seemed to be putting her in his path. Did she really volunteer to work with him? Maybe she wasn't as prickly as she seemed. He thought about the crumpled card from the Hope Tree that was still in his wallet. Anika probably didn't want to work with him but she obviously needed the extra money. Perhaps he'd have a chance to redeem himself in her eyes, help her see that he wasn't trying to be condescending. He really did want to help.

Tayton was explaining something on the ledger and Carlos blinked and refocused, but his thoughts kept wandering to the feisty brunette and her little girl. The project was slated to begin on Monday and he couldn't wait to talk to Anika.

CHAPTER 8

ON MONDAY MORNING, ANIKA WOKE at six-thirty with stiff muscles. She looked out the window and smiled. Who said two feet of snow was such a bad thing? She had taken Megan out to play and started shoveling one of the elderly neighbor's driveway down the street. When the woman offered to pay, Anika had refused, but at the widow's insistence she'd finally accepted and then been hired to shovel the next house. She'd shoveled both of their walks twice and pulled in an extra twenty-five dollars over the weekend. The gray clouds held a promise of more snow, but not enough to shovel again today. That was probably a good thing because Anika's back was sore. She stretched out on the floor and lengthened her spine.

She made a list of the things she needed to pick up at the grocery store before her three o'clock shift at

Kenworth's. This week she was pulling six-hour shifts and the extra money would help to keep the creditors at bay. She closed her eyes and tried to think of something besides bills and paychecks.

A giggle by her ear jolted her awake a few minutes later. She glanced at the clock, fifteen minutes past seven. Okay, it had been almost forty-five minutes. Anika groaned and stretched, snatching Megan and tickling her until the little girl squealed.

Anika laughed and they both collapsed on the floor with a sigh.

"Mommy, are you happy now?" Megan asked.

"I'm trying to be, sweetie. It's just a busy time right now. Lots to do." She ruffled Megan's hair. Her daughter snuggled close to her. Anika pulled the corners of her lips up into a smile. Right up until her mother died, she had said that smiling made you happy even if you weren't. Anika resolved to try it more often, otherwise she'd end up like Cecilia. Megan smiled back at Anika.

Four-year-olds were much more perceptive than people gave them credit for. Anika had tried to hide it, but her daughter noticed the strain that accompanied most days in their cramped apartment. It was hard to shake off the old fears of Jimmy showing up looking for drug money. Anika wasn't sure where he was now, and she wouldn't be surprised if he was back in jail. Thankfully, Megan was too young to remember her deadbeat father and Anika didn't speak of him. It was better that way—

safer that way. She kissed the top of Megan's head. "We'd better cook some breakfast. Who's in the mood for waffles?"

"Me! Me! With extra peaches." Megan jumped up and ran to the kitchen. There was one can of peaches left in the cupboard and Megan had pulled it out by the time Anika followed her into the kitchen. She mixed up the batter while Megan played with some cloth napkins. Anika reached for the cinnamon and her fingers brushed the white sack Reese had given her that still held two chocolate Santas— she was saving them for Megan's stocking as she hadn't been able to find any flaws on the packaging or the chocolate. Why they were marked "no-sale" was beyond her. But Megan couldn't read so she'd have no idea they were free.

Anika shook the cinnamon into the batter and tried to concentrate on the dark flecks of spice instead of the Puerto Rican carpenter/fireman, but she found herself imagining his deep brown eyes again. She whipped the batter until the cinnamon had blended in. She thought about snow, her sore back, Megan's chatter... Anything but Carlos.

CARLOS RUBBED his hands against his jeans. He'd been building up the courage to talk to Anika for the past fifteen minutes. The area for the new soda fountain had been cordoned off with yellow warning tape and Jessica, manager of the women's department had helped him to move all of the stock to another area of the store. Jessica had been pretty friendly but when he'd asked her about Anika, she'd stopped flirting and Carlos could almost see the matchmaker in her head light up. Jessica had left promptly at three when Anika arrived.

It was his responsibility to "interview" the employees he wanted to help with the refurbishing project. Anika would be a hard worker and she was looking for extra opportunities to earn money. He'd overheard her tell Jessica that she could cover her shift on Wednesday. She must have found someone to watch her little girl. That was a good sign that she might accept the extra hours to work with him.

Keira had requested that he do the "noisy work" after hours, so he planned to be at the store until midnight for the next several nights and then early in the morning as well. Hopefully Anika could team up with him and he could get the soda fountain done on time. Of course, he could have asked a man able to heft some weight, but there was only one name on the card that wasn't a female and Carlos was pretty certain that Anika could lift more than the man in his late sixties who was temping in the shoe department.

Carlos blew out a breath and approached the rack of dresses Anika was arranging. She looked up and her eyes widened before she turned and hung up another dress.

"Can I help you?" she asked without making eye contact.

"Actually, yes," Carlos responded.

Anika turned around and yanked another dress off the stand and hung it, forcefully next to the others. She wasn't going to make this easy, so he'd better just get it over with.

"I'm really sorry about the other day," Carlos said. "I didn't mean to embarrass you. Cecilia is hard to deal with. She makes my blood pressure rise and then I do stupid things. I just wanted to help."

Anika licked her lips. "I'm sorry I snapped at you."

Carlos let go of the breath he'd been holding. This was going better than he thought. Maybe she would give him a chance. "I'm in charge of refurbishing the old soda fountain and Cecilia gave me a list of names of employees who might be able to help outside of their shifts." He stopped and gulped for air. There, he'd said it.

Anika paused and he could see her swallow before lifting her eyes to his. The crystal blue color was striking against the dark red of her shirt. This was his chance. If Anika didn't want to work with him, he probably wouldn't have an opportunity to break past her wall made of all brick and steel and prickly thorns. The corners of her eyes crinkled as she studied him. Carlos held out the schedule he'd written up.

"If you want to look it over, you'll see the areas I need

extra help are highlighted in yellow. Keira wants this finished quickly. They're paying fifteen dollars an hour."

The papers crinkled as Anika took them and smoothed them out. She nodded. "I'd like to help, but I don't have much experience in building things."

"That's no problem. I'm a good teacher," Carlos said. His heart thumped when Anika looked up. He shouldn't be so excited to work with someone who had shut him down the way she had last week, but he saw her— the vulnerable side of her that she didn't want him to see. "Most of these things are pretty simple. If you can put together a puzzle, you're qualified to lay tile."

"I put together puzzles with my four-year-old," Anika said. "Does that count?"

Carlos chuckled. "Más o menos. It's a stretch, but I'll take it if that's a yes."

"Yes, I guess it is. Nights work best for me because I'll have a sitter, but I could maybe come in a couple mornings depending on what I can work out for Megan."

"In that case, I might be able to get this finished," Carlos said. "That's a relief."

"Under a lot of pressure, huh?" Anika handed him back the schedule.

"Yeah, I guess the boss is planning some kind of event for the grand reopening to attract more customers." Carlos took the schedules back from Anika and slid them into the folder, but he pulled the top sheet off and held it out. "This copy is for you. Check your schedule and see what you can work out. I'll hope to see you whenever there's a highlighted slot."

"Thanks, Carlos." Anika stepped back to the dress rack, but turned and spoke over her shoulder. "I have a feeling you're trying to help me out again."

"Who me?" Carlos shook his head. "I don't know what you're talking about."

She smiled and turned back to her work.

Carlos walked back to the soda fountain, resisting the urge to turn around and stare at Anika. That had gone better than he expected. The only problem now had to do with the way his heart was pounding when he thought about working alongside Anika. She'd agreed to work with him, but would she consider going on a date? His stomach tightened when he thought about finding the nerve to ask her out. He bent to pick up his bag of tools, thinking about the possibilities in his future. When he looked up a few minutes later, he could have sworn Anika was watching him.

CHAPTER 9

ON HER WAY OVER TO RING UP A CUSTOMER, Anika watched Carlos out of the corner of her eye. His biceps flexed every time he picked up another tool or piece of wood. She'd have to be blind not to notice the way his jeans fit just right, his physique accentuated by the heavy tool belt loaded up with probably ten different tools. She bit her lower lip. Carlos had seemed nervous about asking her to work with him, and she'd almost said no before she started tallying the extra dollars that would be added to her paycheck. It was a dangerous game she was playing. She was supposed to be staying away from the guy, not spending more time with him. So why did her stomach flip every time she thought about working with him?

Maybe it was because he was more than just a good-looking guy. Already, he'd treated her with more respect than Jimmy ever had. Her ex had been handsome, although in a different way. Jimmy never had a hair out of place and always looked carefully put together. That all changed when he started using the drugs he was dealing. Anika shook her head, pushing the memory back. She didn't know if she dared to trust her judgement but her gut was telling her that Carlos was nothing like any of the guys she'd dated before or after Jimmy.

When Anika went to the break room at seven, she met Tayton Wells. Several of the other employees were there and he handed each of them a sheet of paper. "Keira and I have come up with an idea for the holiday selling season. Each week we'll have a friendly competition between the departments in the store. Each department is a team and we expect you to all work together with your department managers to implement ideas that will increase sales over last year." Tayton pointed to a copy of the paper he'd given them. "You can see on this graph that I've recorded the sales for each week from last year along with the target goal and bonus goal for sales this year."

Tayton was well dressed and exuded the professional downtown New York City air, but when he smiled, his face appeared boyish and his eyes twinkled. His dark hair was trimmed above his collar, and the few times Anika had seen him, he'd been clean-shaven and walking at a brisk pace toward his next assignment. "The prize will be store credit of one-hundred and fifty dollars for the winning team," he continued. "If we meet our goal, next week the prize money will go up with a combo of cash and store credit."

Anika sucked in a breath, and straightened in her seat. Money like that would make a huge difference to her and Megan. She surveyed the competition. Jeff was there from housewares, and Tasha from the makeup section, and, she barely stopped from wrinkling her nose, Gentry. Dressed in charcoal suit pants, a button up lavender shirt with a pinstriped vest, Gentry was a perfect model for the men's department but Anika thought he was too shiny. Shiny hair, shiny teeth, and a shiny forehead that she suspected he covered up with powder. He reminded her of how Jimmy was when they first met, preppy and put together. Gentry lounged on the sofa, but he caught her looking and winked at her. Anika turned away and swallowed the funny taste in her mouth.

She turned back to Tayton, paying attention to the last of his speech about holiday competitions. Anika didn't have high hopes of winning, because she didn't work that many hours, but when she considered Jessica's enthusiasm over every detail in the women's department, her lips twitched in a smile. Maybe they'd have a better chance than she originally thought. One hundred and fifty dollars per team at Kenworth's prices, even with the employee discount could only buy a couple things, but they would be high quality and help to make Megan's Christmas a bit brighter.

"Keira explained the contest to the day shift employees earlier. This is a trial run. We'll see how it goes, so have fun with it and see what ideas you can come up with to make Kenworth's *the* place to shop this holiday." Tayton clapped his hands together. "May the best team win."

When Tayton left, Gentry hopped up from the couch and headed toward Anika. She hurried to dial Lila's number before he reached her side. Thankfully, Lila answered.

"Hey, Lila. How is Megan doing?" Anika asked brightly.

"She's asleep now, but she sure was a sweetheart earlier." Lila did a good job of hiding her confusion over Anika's question.

Anika smiled at Gentry and walked away, still talking to Lila. "Hey, do you mind staying until a little after eleven? I have an opportunity to get some extra work on a big project here."

"Sure, I'm working on my history report," Lila's voice was chipper.

"Thanks, I really appreciate it. The store is in a bind and they can use me every night this week so check with your parents and see if that's okay."

"Will do. See you later," Lila said. She sounded excited and that was a relief to Anika. Even though she'd be paying extra babysitting money, the soda fountain renovation might be enough to buy Megan a dollhouse. The one on display at Kenworth's had two stories with little pieces of furniture like a couch, table, and tiny dishes perfect for Barbies, and the few other dolls Megan owned.

Anika walked back out to the floor of the women's section, her eyes immediately searching for and finding Carlos hard at work near the soda fountain. She took a breath and walked over to him. "So, it turns out my sitter can stay late tonight. My shift ends at nine and I can help you until eleven— that is, if you still need me tonight."

Carlos's eyes lit up. "That'd be great."

"I— uh, don't have clothes to change into though." Anika motioned to her favorite red blouse with the silver buttons and her brown dress slacks.

"No problem. We're mostly taking down this old signage, but if you could find an apron or something that might work."

Anika looked over at The Candy Counter. "I bet Reese has an apron she'd let me use."

Carlos nodded. "Good idea."

REESE DID HAVE an extra apron and at two minutes past

nine, Anika tightened the bow behind her back and joined Carlos in front of the old soda fountain bar. He smiled at her when she approached. *He sure is a happy guy*, Anika thought. *Maybe I need to take some lessons.*

"This part is kind of tedious, but it's simple. I need you to take down all of these clips, price tags, and signs." Carlos motioned to the back wall of the soda fountain that had been used to sell various houseware items. There were stockings, stuffed reindeers, and a few Christmas ornaments still on display. He'd moved most of the items earlier and they were stacked in boxes, waiting to be redistributed throughout the store. Anika removed a row of stockings and thought of an idea.

"Maybe I'll put a few of these over in clothing. Our displays need a little pizazz." Anika dropped a few items into a separate box.

"I'm sure that'd be fine," Carlos said. "Jessica helped me earlier and she said Jeff would have to work on restocking this stuff tomorrow."

Anika worked in silence for a few minutes while Carlos used his drill to pull out screws from some of the warped boards on the back of the fountain. She focused on the job of removing the price tags attached to various signs along the large mirror behind the counter, and tried not to look at Carlos. His phone emitted a siren-like tone and she was jolted out of her thoughts.

Carlos grabbed his phone from his tool belt and

studied the screen before texting a response. He slid the phone back into one of the leather straps. "That was notification from the police department."

"Is it a fire?" Anika asked.

"No, just some schedule changes. Sorry to worry you. I have that alarm set for all notifications from them. It works because most of them are calls for accidents or fires," he explained.

"So you help with accidents too? I thought it was just fires."

"The fire truck goes out to all car accidents. It's routine. That's why I'm trained as an EMT." Carlos knelt down next to her and pulled out his measuring tape. "Since Echo Ridge is a small town, the departments work closely together."

"That must keep you pretty busy."

"It's strange, but it kind of comes and goes in spurts. It's like everything happens at once," Carlos said. "One week there won't be anything and the next week, I'll get called out four times."

"That does seem to be how life goes." Anika tugged on a silver bar that had previously held a line of stuffed snowmen. It wouldn't budge so she used both hands, planted her feet, and yanked. The bar came free and she toppled backwards into Carlos. He stumbled, landed on the floor, and Anika fell right into his lap.

"Are you okay?" he asked.

Anika turned her head and then pulled back when she saw how close she was to his face. She felt heat rush into her cheeks. "I'm sorry. You must think I'm a walking accident."

Carlos laughed. "Not at all. Although I'll keep my distance the next time I see you around a Christmas tree."

It was Anika's turn to laugh, and for some reason she giggled which made her self-conscious. She scrambled to get off Carlos and slipped onto the floor, bumping her tailbone. "Ow!"

Carlos helped her up with a chuckle. "Okay, maybe not a walking accident, but a falling one."

"You're not helping." Anika laughed.

"But I'm trying." Carlos cupped her elbow to steady her, and then he dropped his hand and stepped back.

She couldn't be sure, but she thought his skin had a hint of red under his bronze complexion. Anika smiled. It was charming to see Carlos blushing. "Thanks. That was the last one." She pointed to the back wall. "What would you like me to do now?"

"How about we finish clearing out all the miscellaneous stuff from these cabinets?" He pulled open a door on the back side of the soda fountain bar. "I spent a lot of time measuring and drawing up the plans today. Tomorrow night, we should be ready to rip out the broken tiles and start replacing them."

"I'll be sure to bring some old clothes to change into."

"That'd be a good idea," Carlos said. "I'm glad this worked out. How's Megan doing?"

"She's a lot happier when she gets to bed on time. I have a teenage girl watching her." Anika was surprised in a good way that Carlos had remembered Megan's name and asked about her. Most guys avoided the topic of her kid, hoping that if they pretended she was invisible they could flirt without consequences. "Thanks for asking," Anika said.

"Sure, she's a sweet kid. Reminds me of my niece Sylvi," Carlos said. "She's three."

"That's a busy age. Do you have family around here?"

"Most of them are in Florida." Carlos rubbed a cloth over a dusty shelf. "Mi madre doesn't understand why I want to be up here freezing my tail off."

Anika laughed. She loved his accent and how he slipped into a little bit of Spanish when he spoke of his family.

"How about you? Where's your family?"

Anika hesitated. "You know, I don't really have anybody. I was raised by a single mom. She died about eight years ago."

"Man, I'm sorry. That's got to be rough around the holidays."

Normally Anika would bristle at the attention and sympathy, but Carlos sounded sincere. He stopped working and faced her. "I admire you, what you're doing with your daughter. I can tell that it's not easy."

Suddenly everything was blurry and Anika blinked rapidly to clear the moisture in her eyes. There was a knobby lump in her throat trying to burst, but Anika dammed it up and rolled back her shoulders. She swiped a hand over her eyes. "It has been hard, but we're making do."

Carlos nodded. "Mi madre was sick with cancer and mi familia all pitched in to bring her to Florida from Puerto Rico so she could get treatments. I wasn't sure I'd be able to keep my house, but it was all worth it, you know?"

Something was happening inside Anika's chest. That place where her rock-hard heart pumped out a rhythm that protected her and Megan suddenly felt as if a crevice had opened up. Her toes tingled and the lump in her throat doubled in size. Carlos was reaching out to her, allowing her to open up to him if she wanted to. Over the past three years, she'd never been close enough to anyone — male or female— to share her struggles. This man who had a strong family network had just opened up to her, clearly as an invitation to provide a shoulder. And the way he bent over a loose board and pried it up with a crowbar left no doubt that those shoulders were strong. Anika took in a breath. It would be so nice to talk to someone who understood— or even to talk to someone who was willing to listen without judging her for all the things she lacked as a mother, employee, as a person.

"I think that's wonderful what your family did for

your mom." Anika thought about saying more, but the grandfather clock in the housewares department chimed eleven o'clock. "My goodness, I didn't realize it was already so late."

Carlos lifted his head. "The time went by fast tonight." He grinned. "That happens when you work with good people. Let me walk you out to your car and then I'll get cleaned up in here."

"But don't you have to be back in here before seven tomorrow?" Anika tallied the few hours of sleep he'd get and felt the exhaustion hitting her hard.

"It's only for a week. Then I'll have time to recuperate before Christmas." He slid a couple of tools into his belt, and unfastened it from his waist. "Are you parked out back?"

"Yes, but please, I'm fine."

Carlos shook his head. "No, mi madre would be enojado if she found out that I didn't walk a lady to her car at this late hour."

His accent was irresistible. "Okay, you win," Anika said.

They walked back to the employee lounge and grabbed their coats and gloves. When they stepped out of the store, Anika was grateful she'd let him lead her out to the parking lot. The streetlights illuminated some slippery patches of ice and the darkness beyond seemed deeper that night. The subzero air bit at her cheeks and she ducked her head. "It's freezing out here," she mumbled against the fabric of her coat.

"It's nights like these, I can't disagree with mi familia for calling me crazy to live here."

Carlos loved his family, and it sounded like they were close. That was something she'd never had— something she wanted to give to Megan. Anika couldn't wait to get home and kiss Megan's sleeping face.

The light shimmered on a patch of black ice and though she tried to walk carefully, she ended up sliding into Carlos. "They need to salt this before somebody gets hurt." He took her arm and guided her over the slippery asphalt. His heavy, rubber-soled work boots were much steadier on the ice than her dress boots.

"Thank you," Anika said. With his touch, she felt everything come into sharper focus. A magnetic pull was at work between them. Anika couldn't concentrate on anything but the gentle way Carlos moved, his footsteps matching her own in a protective cadence. Her car was parked right next to a puddle that had turned to ice, so she didn't mind when Carlos steadied her as she fished in her purse for the keys.

"Thanks again for helping me, Carlos. I hope you get some rest." She unlocked the door and pulled it open. He held onto it as she slid into her seat.

"Be careful on these roads," he said. "I don't want to get a call from the fire department tonight."

"I will. See you tomorrow." Anika waved and he shut

the door for her. He stood there for a moment while she started the car and pulled out slowly onto the snowy streets. He waved as she drove away. She tried to ignore the tingles creeping up her arm where Carlos had held her. If she didn't need the money so bad, she'd run the other direction because working with Carlos was dangerous for her heart.

CARLOS SLAPPED AT HIS ALARM CLOCK the following morning at six o'clock. Before he even opened his eyes, thoughts of Anika swirled in from every direction. Usually when he was working on a project with a tight timeline like the soda fountain, he'd spend every minute visualizing what he needed to do to transform something old into something new and functional. But all he could see was Anika and the way she looked last night. Her light brown hair pulled back, revealing the slender lines of her neck. Her ivory skin looked soft and her bright blue eyes lit up something inside his chest.

He opened his eyes and stared at the ceiling. There was something special about Anika. Last night it seemed like she was about to open up and talk to him, but then she'd left in a hurry. There was a story behind that beautiful face and Carlos's insides tightened when he thought about the pain behind her eyes. If only she would trust him, he'd show her that there were good men around. Carlos would never hurt a woman and his hands clenched into fists when he thought about the jerk who'd obviously treated Anika terribly.

Carlos hurried to get ready for work, all the while thinking of how he might get up the nerve to ask her on a date. Of course, he didn't know when either of them would have time outside of Kenworth's. He would be working every spare minute on the soda fountain and Anika would be working with him. He'd noticed that her shift at Kenworth's was in the afternoon, so that meant she might have a few minutes free for lunch. He brushed through his hair and stared at himself in the mirror. "You can do this," he told himself. He should have asked her yesterday, but he wouldn't let another day pass.

The thought carried him through the rest of the morning. Work on the soda fountain went quickly. After he secured the area with plastic sheeting to contain the debris, Carlos started working. Not long after, Tayton showed up to help him and with both of them at it, they were able to rip out all of the broken tiles, warped wooden siding, and the ancient laminate flooring before the store opened at ten. Tayton was surprisingly down to earth and the two of them chatted about the direction Kenworth's was taking and the hope that this season would boost them out of the slump they'd been in.

Carlos had several buckets full of debris that he hauled out one by one with the help of a couple of the guys who normally kept the parking lot cleared of snow. If he kept up this pace, he'd have most of the grunt work done before tonight and Anika could help him lay the new tile floor. He whistled until Cecilia walked by with a glare. He couldn't help smiling at the grumpy woman. In just a few hours, Anika would be coming in to start her shift.

Keira Kenworth approached Carlos just before noon. She tucked a strand of strawberry-blonde hair behind her ear and rocked forward onto her toes. "We've come up with a fabulous idea," she held out a flier. "We're going to sponsor an old-fashioned Christmas dance for the grand re-opening of the soda fountain. We're calling it the Candy Cane Twist."

Carlos took the paper and glanced at the date before he reacted. He let out a breath when he saw that it was for the following Saturday. "That's a great idea. And I'll have everything ready before then."

"Terrific, you're doing great with this rush timeline," Keira said. "If possible, we'd like the soda fountain operational by next Thursday so that we can test it out and make sure there isn't anything we haven't thought of. Can we make that deadline?"

"That shouldn't be a problem as long as you get the plumbing done in time," Carlos said. "I've already made a lot of progress today."

"Fantastic. Did Tayton tell you the plumber was coming by today?"

Carlos nodded. "Yeah, I think he should be here any minute."

"Good. Keep up the great work," Keira said. "Oh, and Carlos?"

"Yeah?"

"You should bring a date to the dance. You deserve to have a little fun after all your hard work."

"Uh, I'll think about it," Carlos mumbled. He read the paper again, his eyes catching on the words waltz and jitterbug. He had moves, but wasn't as familiar with the old time dances. But it sure would be neat to take Anika to something like that. He folded the paper and tucked it in his back pocket. Pulling on his gloves, he went back to work removing the final pieces of broken tile and debris from the ailing soda fountain.

A few minutes later he thought he heard Anika's name and he immediately dropped the screwdriver he'd been using to remove screws from the paneling. He was crouched down behind the soda fountain and the two men talking hadn't seen him.

"Anika who?" a man with a deep voice asked.

"You know the new girl over by the sweaters— the one with a nice rack," another man answered.

Carlos peered around the corner and recognized Gentry from men's apparel. Carlos had met him when he repaired the dressing rooms in the men's department last year. Gentry was a creep dressed in nice clothes. Carlos felt his neck heat up with fury at the crass way Gentry was referring to Anika.

The first man laughed. "Well, Keira said not to be shy about inviting co-workers to the dance, since we want to promote positive employee camaraderie."

"Fantastic!" Gentry imitated Keira in a high falsetto. He sniggered "It'll promote more than that."

Both men laughed and walked to the other side of the store. Carlos picked up his hammer and gripped it tightly until his fingertips turned white. There was no way Carlos would let that jerk get near Anika, but what could he do? *I'm going to have to ask her today.* His face burned just thinking about it. What if she said no? That was the likely scenario, but he wanted to make sure that Gentry knew she was unavailable. Maybe he should just tell Gentry to steer clear of her, but that probably wouldn't bode well since Gentry thought he was every woman's Christmas wish.

Carlos sat back on his heels and slipped the hammer back into his tool belt. He could do this. Anika was on the verge of trusting him, and he didn't want to mess this up. He closed his eyes and sent up a prayer, *Please, don't let her get hurt anymore. Help me do the right thing.*

It was hard to concentrate on his work after that. He kept a close eye on the women's department and another eye in the direction of Gentry's area. Carlos knew the moment Anika arrived at her station. He glanced at his watch. It was five past three, only six hours until she'd be working by his side. The flier in his back pocket burned. He had six hours to work up the nerve to ask her to the dance.

Anika's brown hair was pulled back in a ponytail and it swished from side to side as she bent to unload a box of hangers from one of the cupboards near the cash register. She lifted her head and smiled when she saw Carlos watching. He thought about ducking, reminded himself he wasn't in junior high, and waved. She waved back before turning to speak to Jessica who'd just approached pulling a rack of clothes down the aisle.

The work went slower because Carlos kept looking at Anika, and then scolding himself for staring. At seven o'clock, Tayton came out onto the floor and handed out more fliers for the dance. He gave one to Anika, and Carlos watched as she read the flier before dropping it into the trash. Not a good sign.

About thirty minutes later, Carlos heard a familiar voice.

"Hey, where's Anika?" Gentry asked.

Carlos lifted his head and saw Gentry standing in front of Anika's station. Jessica pointed to the back of the store. "She's on break, but she'll be back in about fifteen minutes. What did you want?"

"It's nothing. I'll talk to her when I go on break." He checked his watch before working his way back across the store. Carlos's stomach churned and his palms began to sweat. Anika wouldn't agree to go to the dance with Gentry, would she? The flier in her garbage can indicated she probably wasn't interested, but maybe that's because her automatic response was programmed in because of her history. Carlos had noticed some softening the night before and he'd hoped to approach her when no one else was around. He stood and brushed off his pants. He was on his own time. And it was time for a break.

The employee lounge was quiet since it was almost eight o'clock, only an hour until closing. Carlos spotted Anika in the corner holding a sandwich. She was bent over a magazine in her lap and didn't look up until he was three paces from her.

"Do you mind if I sit here for a minute?" Carlos motioned to the worn green and tan striped sofa.

Anika's eyes widened, she scooted to the edge, and nodded. "There's plenty of room."

She's already acting nervous, Carlos thought. He sucked in a breath and sat down. Remembering the way Gentry talked about Anika gave Carlos courage to do what needed to be done. It was probably best to just get it over with. He opened his mouth to speak, but Anika turned toward him. "I haven't seen you in here before. I wondered if you ever stopped for a break."

"I— well, once in a while I stop for a breather." He leaned back against the sofa. Maybe if he pretended he was relaxed, she would too. "Things are coming along nicely today. I thought you might be glad to know that I got a lot of the dirty work done." He brushed at the dust on his pants.

"I brought my work clothes. I'm not afraid of a little dirt." Anika quirked an eyebrow.

Carlos smiled at her jab, but he was having trouble concentrating with that piece of paper in his pocket. "Uh, I guess Tayton told you about the dance they're doing for the grand re-opening of the soda fountain?"

"Yeah, that's kind of a neat idea," Anika said. "Are you worried about getting everything done on time?"

"No," Carlos answered. "Keira checked with me earlier and I told her we could do it." He hesitated after using the word "we" because he hadn't meant to imply he and Anika. "The plumber came in and got started. He'll finish up his work tomorrow."

"That's good." She finished off her sandwich and brushed her hands together.

Carlos scrambled to think of something to say. *Crap, her break is almost up.* It was now or never. "I wondered if you'd like to go to the dance with me?" His voice caught on the last word and he cleared his throat, but kept eye contact.

Anika looked down. "That's nice of you, but I can't."

"So you're not going to go at all? Or were you hoping someone else might ask you?" Carlos kept his tone friendly and innocent.

She shook her head. "I don't like being away from Megan more than necessary."

"I understand," Carlos said. His shoulders slumped, but he decided to try one last thing. "You know, I bet she'd have a blast if you brought her along."

Anika's head lifted and she gave Carlos a genuine smile. "That's sweet of you to think of her."

Carlos grinned back. Maybe this wouldn't be so bad after all, but then Anika's smile dissolved into the worry lines around her mouth. "But I can't. Thanks so much for asking me. I'll see you later."

Before he could think of a response, she stood and hurried out the door. Carlos slumped back against the sofa and heaved a sigh. At least he had tried. He wasn't prepared for how much Anika's rejection stung. Even as he tried to reassure himself that she wasn't really turning him down, more the situation, he couldn't shake the foreboding feeling that he might've messed up his chances for any kind of date with Anika by rushing forward.

He slammed his fist into the cushion wishing it was Gentry's face. That made his heart pound because Anika had left and would probably run right into Gentry. Carlos nearly ran from the employee lounge. He skidded around the corner, barely missing a customer. By the time he reached the women's department, his heart was triple-timing the beats and his nerves felt loaded with electricity. Gentry wasn't in sight, but neither was Anika.

ANIKA SAT DOWN ON THE FLOOR with a pile of socks and began sorting them into the correct bins. "I hate Christmas time," she grumbled.

"Sweetheart, you need to lighten up!" Jessica said. She was probably the only person in Echo Ridge who could say that and make it sound like your best friend had just given you a hot fudge brownie sundae. Anika hadn't seen her behind the racks of silky pajamas, but her manager must have heard her Scrooge-like statement.

"Really, I mean it." Jessica moved aside a rack of clothes to face Anika. "You're in this slump and you walk around like the world is out to get you." She held out the flyer to the Candy Cane Twist. "You need to give the world another chance. And while you're at it, give Carlos Rodriguez a chance too."

Anika's head snapped up. "What?"

Jessica giggled. "I was right." She gave a little fist pump. "Girl, take it from me. If Carlos is paying attention to you, he's not just flirting and you'd better think really hard before turning him down."

Anika opened her mouth and closed it again.

"Wait, did he already ask you to the dance?" Jessica's face morphed "You didn't! Please tell me you did not turn Carlos Rodriguez, finest fireman in Echo Ridge, down."

"I told him I couldn't go." Anika sighed.

Jessica groaned. "Anika, this isn't right. You have to fix this."

"I can't," Anika said. "What's the point? I'd just be wasting my time. No guy wants to be strapped with a woman like me no matter how sweet my daughter is."

"Did you say, what's the point?" Jessica bit her knuckles. "Have you ever walked behind Carlos? I mean, if there was a mold for the perfect— "

"Okay, okay. You've made *your* point," Anika interrupted her. "He's totally hot, but I can't afford to get involved with anyone right now."

"It's one date, not a proposal," Jessica said. "C'mon, we'll all be there. You can't miss it. And hey, it'd be a good opportunity to show that you're a team player. You know, that you're serious about being considered for the full-time position after the holidays."

Anika sighed. She was about to shake her head but she had a feeling that Jessica wasn't going to take no for an answer. "I'll go and talk to him."

"And be nice," Jessica said.

"I'll try," Anika replied.

"What is it with the women in this town?" Jessica grumbled. "It's like they're all wearing full body armor. Cupid doesn't have a chance."

Anika laughed. "I'll see you later." She stuffed the last of the socks in the bin and walked toward the checkout stand. She saw movement to her left in the lingerie section and stopped. There was no one there, but she could have sworn she'd seen Gentry in his purple silk shirt out of the corner of her eye. A long red nightgown swung back and forth as if it had just been bumped. *Strange.* Anika shrugged and continued walking. There was another flier for the Candy Cane Twist on the counter. She studied the details about the dance Jessica had insisted she attend. She wasn't sure if she even had anything to wear to the dance. Carlos came to her mind. The hurt look in his eyes had her clenching the paper. She stuffed it in her purse and buried herself in her work. The countdown to Christmas was in full swing and there was plenty to do at Kenworth's to keep her busy.

WHEN CARLOS FINALLY FOUND GENTRY, he was walking away from the lingerie section of the women's department and his face was red. Carlos nodded at him as they passed, but Gentry didn't make eye contact. It looked like Anika had turned him down too. At least one thing had gone right that day. He wasn't giving up on Anika. Tonight he'd show her that he really did care about her and her daughter Megan. Maybe he could ask her to lunch tomorrow.

By the time Anika showed up to help him at the Soda Fountain, Carlos had rehearsed about fifty different conversations in his mind. None of them had infused the confidence he needed to approach her again. He handed her a pair of work gloves. "So you won't get your hands dirty."

She laughed and slapped his arm with the gloves. She set them on the counter and tilted her head, puckering her lips slightly. "So, I'm thinking about going with you to the dance."

"You are?" Carlos's mouth hung open. "I mean, that's great." He stood up straighter and stepped closer to her. The way she'd been standing there with her lips just begging to be kissed had him all undone. Heat rose up in his belly, and he blinked, trying to clear his thoughts.

"I'm really sorry about the way I acted," Anika said. "This is hard for me. I have trust issues."

Carlos nodded. She was talking to him, and he didn't want to mess this up. He thought about every lecture his mother had given him on listening to girls and looked straight into Anika's beautiful crystal blue eyes. His mind whirred with some of the conversations he'd practiced earlier. *Just be you*, he thought.

"It's okay. I'm not very good at this either." Carlos rubbed his hand along the edge of the countertop. "I wanted to ask you to lunch first, you know, give you a chance to get to know me, but I was afraid that someone else was going to ask you to the dance first."

Anika actually smiled at him. "That's sweet of you, but I doubt anyone else would ask me."

"How is it that you don't see yourself? You're gorgeous, and a good mother too." Carlos brushed his fingers across her knuckles.

She looked at her hand, curled her fingers inward, and then relaxed them. "No, I'm not. I'm a terrible mother. I can't even pay my daycare bill so I brought Megan to work and almost got fired over it. She's only four and I'm already letting her down."

"She looked pretty happy when I saw her." Carlos kept his hand over hers. "Just because your situation doesn't look like the perfect scenario doesn't mean you aren't doing your best."

Anika hung her head and sniffed. Uh-oh, she wasn't supposed to cry. What should he do now? The urge to take her into his arms was strong, but he didn't want to mess this up. "I'm sorry. I didn't mean to pry," he mumbled.

"No, it's not that." Anika sniffed again. "I just don't know what to do."

The magnetic pull between them was too much. Carlos stepped forward and wrapped his arms around her tentatively. She leaned into him, her head resting against his chest, her body trembling. He held her for a moment, breathing in the scent of her— vanilla and cinnamon. Anika smelled like his favorite cup of Christmas cocoa. He wondered what her lips would taste like. Before he could follow that train of thought, Anika stepped back and wiped her eyes. He wished he could keep holding her, somehow make her believe that the way he saw her was true. She was a good woman. He reached out and wiped a single tear from her cheek.

Her cheeks flushed and she ducked her head. "I'm sorry. I think I'm really worn out." She fished a tissue out of her pocket and dabbed at her eyes. "It's a stressful time of year."

"And Cecilia coming down on you doesn't help," Carlos added. "Try to let it go. She's like that with everyone."

"Even you?"

Carlos chuckled. "Especially me. I've learned to anticipate her complaints. She could find something wrong with Santa Claus given the chance. I think she missed her calling in life."

Anika giggled. "What's that?"

"She should have worked for the IRS or something." Carlos brushed a bit of sawdust off the ledge of the soda fountain. "Look, if you're too tired to work tonight, it's okay. I'm actually ahead of schedule."

Anika considered for half a second. "If I promise not

to blubber on you anymore will you let me work with you for an hour?"

"That sounds great, but you can uh, talk to me anytime." He nudged the stack of tiles with his toe. "How about we finish laying this row tonight?"

"I can do that."

They worked alongside each other, and the process went smoother than Carlos had ever remembered. The gleaming tiles in a mint green shade lined up perfect next to the white squares on the grid he'd prepared. Anika told him more about Megan, and he shared a few stories from his early years in Puerto Rico.

At ten-thirty, Carlos's watch chirped, and he set down the last tile in the row. "I've kept you past your bedtime. It's already been an hour and a half."

"That's okay," Anika said. "This is just what I needed." She moved the tile an eighth of an inch to the left.

Carlos noticed her attention to detail and nodded. She was a perfect partner to work with, eager to learn, and with an eye for what needed to be done. More than that, she was excellent company. He wanted Anika in his arms again, snuggled against his chest. His heart thrummed when he breathed in her scent lingering in the air around them. If she would agree to go on a real date with him, maybe she could see that he really did want to know more about her. "I was serious when I said I wanted to take you to lunch. How about a date tomorrow — me, you, and Megan?"

Anika lifted her head, blue eyes dancing. "I almost said no, but I don't want to face Jessica's wrath tomorrow if she finds out I turned you down twice."

"Jessica? What does she have to do with this?"

"Well, she might've threatened me when she heard I turned you down for the dance."

Carlos raised an eyebrow. "So, does that mean you're saying yes to lunch?"

She brushed her hands on her jeans and stood. "Yes. I think that'd be really nice. My shift starts at three."

Carlos had her shift memorized, but he didn't say so. "Are you a fan of Chip's Diner? They serve the best fish and chips in town."

"I've heard of that place, and Megan loves fries."

"Can I pick you up at noon?"

"Uh, how about we meet you there?" Anika said. "I have a few errands to run before."

"It's a date." Carlos wondered if Anika was embarrassed about where she lived. She had mentioned they were in walking distance of the library and there were some pretty rundown apartments near there. His chest tightened. Anika was a hard worker, trying to do right by her daughter. She deserved better. He licked his lips. He'd made a few phone calls already. He prayed that the local Christmas foundation would be able to deliver a miracle to Anika and Megan this year.

ANIKA FELT LIKE EVERY CHILDHOOD memory of the night before Christmas, stomach churning with anticipation. But Santa didn't have anything to do with her jitters, a certain carpenter with strong hands and a kind smile had her spinning around her apartment primping like it was the first day of high school all over.

She curled her hair and clipped it back so it hung loose over her shoulders. Kenworth's gave the employees a discount and she had found a blue rayon blouse on the clearance rack for only three dollars and fifty cents. With the extra money from the soda fountain, she'd gone ahead and splurged considering it her Christmas gift to herself. It hung nicely over her blue jeans and she practiced smiling to see if some of her worry lines would decrease. She smoothed her fingers over the scowl line in between her eyes. Maybe Jessica was right, it was time for her to lighten up. She was stepping way out of her comfort zone to go on this date with Carlos.

Megan bounced around the room. "Hamburgers, hamburgers, hamburgers, and fries!"

"No hamburgers or fries until you hold still long enough to let me braid your hair." Anika scooped up Megan and headed for the bathroom. She tickled her and the little girl squealed.

"You're the French fry monster, Mommy!" Megan giggled.

"Okay, hold still, sweetheart." Anika brushed through Megan's flyaway hair and braided it quickly while her daughter squirmed. She couldn't remember the last time they'd eaten at a real diner. Megan would make a new memory today— that was worth going out on one date with Carlos. Although the Candy Cane Twist next week would make two dates, but the thought didn't scare Anika as much as it had before.

At five minutes after twelve, Anika pulled up to Chip's Diner. Megan giggled and pointed at the big red rooster perched on top of the diner. Carlos must have been waiting right inside because he hurried out and opened her car door. "Hi, how's Megan today?" he waved at Megan buckled into the back seat.

"We're great. I hope you didn't have to wait long," Anika said.

"I just put our name down for a table, so your timing is perfect." He reached out his hand to help her from the car. Anika took it and what felt like a spark ran from his fingertips to hers. She let go and turned to unbuckle Megan.

"This is my friend Carlos I told you about. He's going to buy you a hamburger."

Megan tilted her head, studying Carlos. "And French fries?"

Carlos laughed. "Lots of French fries."

Megan hopped out of the car and stood next to her mother. The three of them walked inside the diner together. Chip's Diner was probably as old as the two buddies in their nineties sharing a table right inside the door. A hostess wearing a light yellow dress and a name tag of Bettie led them to one of the booth seats flanking the window. Anika took in the aroma of bacon, coffee, steak fries and milkshakes that hung heavy in the air. Her stomach rumbled while they looked over the menu. After they ordered, Anika helped Megan color her kids menu.

"This is a nice place," Anika said. "I've heard a lot about it, but I've only been once— when I applied for a job."

"Well, I'm glad you didn't get that job or we wouldn't have met," Carlos said.

For some reason Anika felt her cheeks grow warm. She smiled. "Me, too."

Carlos reached his hand across the booth table and

covered hers. Immediately her whole body was alert with his touch. "Do you have the same work schedule next week?"

"Yep. Three to nine except for the days I'm closing, then I have to stay a little later. What about you? What's next after the soda fountain?"

"I'm not scheduled to do any more projects at Kenworth's and most everybody is getting ready for Christmas so I'm hoping to spend some time on my own place. It's a fixer-upper."

"Do you like doing renovation?" Anika asked.

"I do. It's a challenge and it's hard to be patient while I wait for the money to complete each project, but I've been working on the house for a year and it's really coming along."

"Carlo, can I have my French fries yet?" Megan said his name without the -s.

Carlos leaned over the table. "I think they're cooking them right now so be careful when they bring them out to you, they'll be nice and hot. You don't want to burn your little fingers."

Megan turned her hand over and studied her fingers, looked up at Carlos and smiled. "I'm hungry for fries."

Anika and Carlos laughed. The waitress brought out their food and Anika kept busy helping Megan while they continued to chat.

"I'd love to show you my house sometime, if you'd

like." Carlos dipped two fries in ketchup and popped them in his mouth.

"That would be great." Anika's feet tingled. Carlos wanted to see her again, and she was okay with that, eager almost to spend more time with him.

"How about next week, maybe Monday? We could do lunch at my place." Carlos leaned forward, his eyes bright with excitement.

Anika was about to say yes, but then she thought about how she was supposed to have sworn off men. Carlos had found his way past her barrier and even though she liked him, a buzzing in her head reminded her of all the bad memories Jimmy had helped store away — memories that impacted the choices she made today. "Maybe we should see how things go with the soda fountain first. I don't want to overbook you."

Carlos's smile slipped for a fraction of a second, but he recovered quickly. "Probably a good idea."

"I'll see you tonight though," Anika said.

"I have my extra pair of gloves ready so you won't have to get your hands dirty."

Anika laughed. Carlos had a way of turning every situation into something to smile about. She felt bad for turning down his offer to see his house. Her insides were jumbled up like the twisting branches of the giant artificial Christmas tree she'd had to decorate. If she could make it through the holidays unscathed, it would be a small miracle. The way Carlos was flirting with her, and how her heart was responding to his every look and touch should have excited her, but the doubts kept circling around in the back of her mind. Caution had been her constant companion over the past few years, so why did she feel like running into Carlos's waiting arms?

CHAPTER 13

*A*NIKA FELT LIKE SKIPPING TO WORK after her lunch date with Carlos. Even Lila noticed something different about her attitude when she came to babysit Megan.

"Good news about your job?" Lila asked just before Anika was leaving.

Anika shrugged. "Sort of. The extra hours are great, but I still don't know if this temp job has a chance of turning into something permanent."

"I'll keep my fingers crossed for you because I've got more homework done in the past week than I have all year." Lila tapped the pile of books on the kitchen table.

"That's good. Make sure you save your money for college. Then when you get old like me you won't have to worry about working temp jobs." Anika smiled to soften the hard truth of her words.

Lila nodded. "I will. I'm going to be a teacher."

"You'd be excellent at that." Anika waved before she opened the door. Lila beamed and distracted Megan as Anika scooted out into the winter wonderland of her parking lot. She hated scraping her windshield, but with the temperatures hovering below freezing for the last couple days everything was like a solid sheet of ice. Her Nissan took a few minutes to warm up so Anika was nearly to Kenworth's by the time heat started to blow from the shuddering vents.

Even though she probably should resist, she made a detour and walked past the soda fountain on her way to the women's department. Carlos lifted his head in a nod toward Anika. "Hi again."

"Fancy seeing you here," she said.

He lifted one shoulder. "This place is kind of growing on me. Kenworth's has great employees."

"See you later." Anika wanted to stand there and talk with him, to feel the warmth emanating from his dark chocolate brown eyes, but she walked purposely to her station and checked the notes Jessica had left for what needed to be done first.

Re-stock the Christmas display. Great idea, Anika! We're in the lead! —Jessica

Anika reread the note twice before tucking it away with a smile. Their department was in the lead for the sales contest! She walked around the counter to re-stock the display. Jessica was right, the Christmas stockings and glittery sweaters were selling like ice water in the desert. Anika had worried over what Jessica would think about her idea, but it had been a great choice to set up a display of Christmas décor alongside the sweaters and fancy dresses people would wear to Christmas parties during December.

The stockings, bells, and ornaments she'd taken from the houseware section still rung up the same in the women's department and it seemed to be helping people remember what they needed to get ready for Christmas. It had provided extra exercise for Anika because she'd had to return to housewares four times already to restock her display. She put a stuffed reindeer next to a pile of long sleeved blouses and hung another stocking from the edge of the table.

After she set up everything, she walked through the Children's department, eyeing the rows and rows of beautiful clothing, blankets, and toys— lots of well-made toys. If they won the sales contest, she wouldn't have to buy the cheap dollar store crap to stuff Megan's stocking. Anika found the doll section and sighed when she saw the three-story dollhouse on display. Megan had found it the first day she came to the store and subsequently told Santa all about it. "It's easy, Santa. You can get it right from this store. The elves won't even have to make it."

Santa had laughed a genuine Ho, ho, ho, but Anika had looked away before either of them could see the pain in her eyes. But now, it might just be a possibility.

By Friday morning, Carlos could feel every muscle in his tired body screaming at him for a rest. He and Anika had worked late again last night laying the last of the tile behind the soda fountain counter. Carlos would seal it late Saturday night. Hopefully most of the smell would be gone by Monday morning. There was still a lot of work to do installing new cabinetry, barstools, and lights but with Anika's help, everything should be finished by next Thursday in time for the dance on Saturday.

He kneaded out the tension in his neck and his mind wandered toward Anika again. She'd turned down his offer for another lunch date, but he wasn't going to give up. He liked her, and he was almost certain the feeling was mutual but Anika was too scared to consider more than a date.

"Carlos, I was looking for you," Cecilia said as she approached, interrupting his daydreams.

"Here I am." He resisted the urge to say something like, *where else would I be?* He was surprised to see her; she'd been out of his range lately, which had been nice.

"I'm concerned that you aren't going to have this project done in time," Cecilia's tone was smug, as if she'd expected him to fail all along.

He gave her his best fake smile. "Actually, things are right on schedule."

"Oh?" Cecilia tapped her foot against the new tile.

"This doesn't look like the tile we picked out. Do you still need to replace it?"

Carlos had hoped she wouldn't notice, but he should've known better. The specific tile requested for the soda fountain had been on back-order so he made the decision to purchase one that was almost identical. Chances were that Keira would say it was just fine, especially because the replacement tile was on sale but Carlos hadn't seen her yet. He had planned on asking forgiveness for making the decision.

"Actually, we had to make a change of plans to have everything ready in time. I'll be sealing this tile over the weekend." He didn't want to present an opening for Cecilia to nitpick so he talked a little bit faster. "Keira and Tayton told me the most important thing was to be done on time. I'm sure that they will be fine with the slight change in texture of the tile."

"That's betting on a lot, possibly your job." Cecilia leaned over to inspect the tile. "It's not just the texture. The color is off too."

Carlos bristled at her remark. She may hand him the paycheck but Keira was the one in charge of the soda fountain renovation. He kept silent a few beats, trying to figure out the game Cecilia was playing. He wasn't going to play mouse to her cat. She finally straightened and looked at him. "This isn't acceptable."

"I disagree. This tile saves the company money and it matches the countertop better. Since the tile is already installed, it's a moot point. Now, if you'll excuse me, I'll get back to work." Carlos walked away from Cecilia to the other side of the counter.

"With an attitude like that, you can take Kenworth's off your list of clients," Cecilia spat.

Carlos furrowed his brow. "What is wrong with you?" The words came out before he could stop them and he saw their effect on her face.

She narrowed her eyes and her sunken cheeks appeared even more pinched. "Nothing that a few changes of employees can't fix." She stormed off, her heels clicking along the aisle toward her office in the back of the store. Carlos stood there for a second, stunned at what had just occurred. Cecilia had always been moody and sullen, but her hidden Grinch must be on full alert. He sighed. Hopefully Keira and Tayton would be able to see past Cecilia's doom and gloom to the fine job he'd been doing on the soda fountain. If not, he might have to hold onto his cash instead of investing it in remodeling his bathroom. He clenched his hammer, wishing there was something to demolish right then. His next thoughts were of Anika. If Cecilia was on the rampage, he prayed that Anika could steer clear of her.

CHAPTER 14

ANIKA LOOKED FOR CARLOS when she came in to start her shift, but he was nowhere in sight. She scrubbed her foot against the mat behind the counter in the women's department, surprised at how much just the sight of him lifted her mood. It wasn't possible to think about that long because the Friday afternoon shoppers were clogging up every aisle of Kenworth's. It seemed that the promotions Keira and Tayton had planned were doing well.

At five minutes to seven, Anika took her break. She walked over to the Soda Fountain— Carlos still wasn't there. Her shoulders slumped. She turned to go and stumbled into Cecilia. "Oh, excuse me," Anika said. "I didn't see you there."

"Are you the one who has been taking items from housewares and setting them up in the women's *clothing* department?" Cecilia demanded, ignoring Anika's apology and aptly jumping down her throat.

Anika stepped back, steadying herself against the edge of the soda fountain. "Yes, they've been selling really well and almost everyone has bought from our holiday line at the same time." Anika hoped that her reasoning would get through to Cecilia, but the woman's eyebrows remained pointed as if they'd been starched into that angry slant.

"Every item in this store has to be accounted for and Jeff over in housewares is missing several items. He hasn't been able to total out for days." Cecilia pointed at the display of stockings and sweaters. "I'm afraid that if we don't get this problem solved, there will be pay cuts all around. Merchandise has to be paid for."

Anika gaped. Was she being accused of stealing when all she'd done was move around a few items? Panic wound its way up her throat. "But, wait," Anika protested. "That doesn't make sense. All of our computers are connected. It doesn't matter where an item rings up, the computer accounts for it." Her mind raced. All she'd done was sold items— lots of items. She remembered the challenge Tayton had given them on Monday to up their sales. Jessica had said they were in the lead. Anika looked past Cecilia to see Jeff's balding head behind the counter in housewares. So that's what this was all about. Jeff was obviously falling behind, but he should have been doing better because everyone was purchasing houseware items in the women's department. Anika pressed her lips into a thin line. That jerk had told on her to try to win the bonus Tayton had offered. Anika narrowed her eyes and refocused on Cecilia's gravelly tone. She would not lose her job over a stupid contest.

"Christmas is a busy time. A hard time for everyone," Cecilia continued. "It puts a lot of pressure on people and they do things they otherwise wouldn't."

"No, stop." Anika held up her hand. "I haven't done anything wrong. I've sold almost one-hundred stockings in the last week and I'm sure Jeff is upset because he isn't meeting his goals even though my department has been helping him. But accusing someone of stealing to try to win a stupid contest isn't worth it. You can go right back over to Jeff and tell him he can have the prize."

Cecilia stopped, her mouth hanging open. "He— uh, I— you'll have to excuse me for a moment." She stomped off toward housewares leaving Anika with a stomach full of boulders. This probably wouldn't end well.

AFTER A COUPLE HOURS HAD PASSED, Anika started to relax, hopeful that the situation with Jeff and Cecilia had been resolved. At six-forty-five, Anika was paged into Cecilia's office and she shook her head at her own hopeful stupidity. Cecilia was obviously out for blood. The office was the opposite of cozy, with an ugly metal desk, harsh overhead light, and an annoying clicking noise that the printer emitted every few seconds. Anika's hands shook and she smoothed them in her lap when she sat down. Cecilia looked like a stiff board, sitting erect in her office chair.

"I talked with Jeff at length and we examined all the sales records. I even had Tayton take a look. We were able to find an error in the reporting." She paused lifting her chin a fraction of an inch. Anika tried not to look at her flaring nostrils. Something had Cecilia upset, but Anika couldn't think of anything she'd done to warrant execution. The look Cecilia gave her made the hangman's noose look friendly. "Everything has been accounted for and the sales total showed a clear winner."

Anika held her breath. Maybe Cecilia was going to deliver good news.

"Tasha at the fragrance counter sold twenty percent more than all of the other departments in the store. She has been awarded the store credit."

Anika slumped against the back of the chair. Visions of Megan cheering in delight over a dollhouse vaporized before her. It had only been a chance, one that Anika had hoped for too hard. She closed her eyes, *when would she ever learn?* Every time she hoped, it betrayed her. The silence stretched on, and Anika opened her eyes. Cecilia was waiting for her to say something. "Oh, that's nice," was all she could manage.

"I'm very concerned about the problems you're causing here at Kenworth's," Cecilia said.

"What do you mean?" Anika sat upright, leaning on the edge of her chair.

"Picking fights with other employees, flirting on the job. Really Anika, I thought you were interested in making this job permanent. Apparently, I was wrong."

Anika felt like Cecilia had just slammed her fist into her stomach. The air whooshed out of her, but she gulped and spoke rapidly. "Please. I haven't caused any problems. I'm on time for my shifts. I've covered other people's shifts and worked extra. I didn't pick a fight. What did you expect me to do when Jeff accused me of stealing?"

Cecilia huffed. "Calm down. No one accused you of stealing."

Anika scrunched her eyebrows together thinking of all the times she'd let Jimmy bully her into giving up her money for his habit, the begging she'd had to do to keep this job, the way she had scrimped and scraped for the last few years— it was too much. This wasn't the woman she was before she met Jimmy. Somewhere along the way, he'd made her believe she wasn't worth fighting for. Well, Carlos had shown her that she was. Only, she was the one who needed to do the fighting. She pulled back her shoulders. "Actually you did. I understood your meaning clearly and now you're angry that Tayton proved you wrong."

"Well, that's—" Cecilia started but Anika interrupted her.

"But you're right, too. I do want to work at Kenworth's. I think it's a great store. It represents the heart of Echo Ridge. But don't expect for one minute that I will be less than honest and hard-working. I'm not going to tell you anything to brown-nose and I never have."

Cecilia sputtered. "That's enough. If we weren't short-handed, I'd let you go right now. As it is, you will stop working with Carlos Rodriguez. I have reports that you're spending most of the time flirting. We may be pulling someone else in to finish the renovation, so we no longer need your help. This meeting is finished."

Anika stood and glared at Cecilia. She and Carlos had worked hard late into the night. Sure, they were friendly but she wasn't taking advantage of the company's time. "I haven't done anything wrong and if you continue to harass me, I'll report you to the temp agency. I'm not afraid of you anymore." She spun on her heel and left the office. The door clicked shut harder than she'd intended making her wish she could go back and slam it for good measure.

The store hummed with energy, every department looked busy. It probably wasn't the best time for a break, but since Anika already had someone covering her station, she decided to take a moment to settle her heart so it didn't jump out of her chest. She was angry, slightly awed by her own bravery, and on the verge of tears.

Inhaling slowly, Anika tried to clear her mind of the knife Cecilia had just slammed into her coffin. There weren't any other jobs available in Echo Ridge like Kenworth's. Lila was a huge lifesaver and if Anika had to work during a different time, she would lose her affordable babysitter. The extra hours she'd been working with Carlos weren't a lot, but it was enough to pay her heat bill that had skyrocketed with the plummeting temperatures. She rubbed a hand across her face, trying to hold the tears back. Now wasn't the time, she could cry later. Anika took another deep breath and walked into the employee lounge. She almost turned around when she saw Gentry next to the fridge drinking a Coke, but he had already spotted her.

"Hey, Anika. You're doing pretty well in your department, aren't you?" Gentry set down his drink and crossed the room.

Anika shrugged, she wasn't going to share any details with him. "I'm keeping busy." She didn't like Gentry. It was always a strange phenomenon when you met someone and immediately didn't like them. But Gentry, with his perfectly pressed clothing, manicured nails, and highlighted hair, rubbed her the wrong way.

She found herself comparing the higher pitch of Gentry's voice to Carlos's rich voice— the way he'd whispered in her ear made her shiver. She ducked her head to hide the smile of her memory of Carlos.

"I heard you're having some trouble with Jeff," Gentry said.

That caught her attention. Anika narrowed her eyes and studied Gentry, not sure if he was acting the part of friend or foe. "I think it's all taken care of now." But she didn't think that. She was trying not to imagine how things didn't seem like they could possibly get worse when Gentry took a step closer to her.

He raised his eyebrows. "Oh, I wouldn't be too sure about that. I think Jeff has some other plans up his sleeve."

Anika cocked one hip and put her hand on it. "Like I told Cecilia, I don't care about the stupid contest." But she did care, that extra money could buy Megan's Christmas. The doll house in the children's section at Kenworth's was fifty-nine dollars and even though it was made of flimsy materials, it was Anika's only option. If she didn't win the sales contest next week, she wouldn't have enough to buy it.

"Hey, you should totally win the contest. Sorry, that came out wrong. I meant to say that you should watch out where Jeff is concerned." He leaned in and lowered his voice. "I think he's going to try to ruin one of your displays."

Anika straightened, and stepped away from Gentry. His cologne was too strong, and because she recognized it as one of the most expensive scents from the fragrance counter, she immediately hated it. "What are we, in third grade?"

Gentry lifted his hands as if to ward off an attack. "I'd like to help. Don't shoot the messenger."

Anika barely contained an eye-roll. "How can *you* help me?"

Gentry lifted one shoulder and swiveled so that he stood right next to Anika. "Jeff and I are on good terms — he might even say friends. I could tell him to back off and quit messing with my girl." He hip-bumped Anika, winking at her. "If he knew you were going to the Candy Cane Twist with me, I could be persuaded to have a conversation with the man."

Anika stepped away from Gentry, her hand rubbing along her hip. He was weird. He'd actually hip-bumped her, and now he was trying some kind of morphed blackmail to get her to go to a stupid Christmas dance? "I'm already going to the dance with Carlos."

"I know, but you could always change your mind if you had a good enough reason, right?" Gentry smiled, but it appeared like the sparkling edge of a knife to her.

Anika took another step back. He already knew she was going with Carlos? She barely suppressed a shudder. "I need to get back to work." She looked past Gentry's shoulder to the doorway. "I'm sure we both have quite a few customers out there."

He closed the distance between them and put his

hands on her arms. "Anika, why won't you give me a chance? I'm a great guy and I want to help you."

She tried to shrug away from him, but he tightened his grip on her arms. "Let go of me."

"Please, just consider going on one date with me. I can tell Jeff to back off, you can get to know me, and we'll all have a Merry Christmas." There was a note of desperation in his voice that set off all kinds of warning bells in Anika's head.

"No, thank you. Gentry, I can't." She stated it firmly and kindly, looking him directly in the eye.

"Can't or won't?" Gentry asked, and though she didn't think it was possible, he moved even closer. His breath warmed her cheek as he leaned toward her. "You can still change your mind."

"Hands off the lady," Carlos spoke from behind Gentry, his voice full of fury.

Gentry startled, letting go of Anika and she jumped back. She continued moving backward as Gentry turned toward Carlos. "Hey, we were just talking dude."

"You're done talking. Get back to work." Carlos pointed at the door.

"Whatever," Gentry said.

Carlos grabbed Gentry's arm, and Anika saw his fingers tighten. "No, it's not whatever. It's time to get back to your station. You don't need to be in here. Your break is over."

Gentry winced. His eyes hardened and he stepped

back. When Carlos took another step in his direction, Gentry retreated quickly from the room.

Anika's body trembled. She sucked in a breath. Carlos turned and put his arms around her. "I hope you don't mind that I interfered, but that guy was ticking me off."

Anika reached her arms around Carlos and hugged him. "Thank you. I don't mind at all. He was totally out of line."

Carlos looked down at her and she glanced at his lips, her heart pounded at his closeness. The arc of energy between them sizzled and she let herself indulge for half a second, wondering what it would be like to kiss him. Then she remembered that she was still at work. She stepped back but Carlos reached for her hand as she moved them from around his waist.

"At first I wasn't sure what was going on, until I saw your face or I would've acted even faster." He rubbed his thumb over her knuckles. She wanted to melt into his arms again.

"Oh, you mean the look like I was about to vomit on Gentry?"

Carlos laughed. "Something like that."

Anika put her other hand on his arm. "Thank you. It's been so stressful. Cecilia is totally on my case."

"I'm sorry. That's why I came looking for you. I thought I heard you paged to the back."

"Yes, and then I thought I might take a break to

settle down." Anika shook her head. "That didn't work either."

"It probably won't make you feel better, but she essentially fired me this morning."

"What? She can't do that," Anika said.

Carlos pulled his bottom lip through his teeth. "She was really upset that I changed the tile for the Soda Fountain, but I think she was just looking for some way to sabotage me. She has a personal vendetta against every person in this store."

"I can't stand her. She told me if we weren't short-handed I'd be fired too, and she said there were reports that I've been flirting with you and I'm not supposed to work with you anymore." Anika's face felt warm as she divulged the accusations Cecilia had pinned on her.

Carlos furrowed his brow. "It doesn't make sense."

"I know. I'm trying not to feel panicked, but earlier today she implied that I was stealing."

"That's getting way out of hand. We need to talk to Keira. How could she even accuse you of something like that?"

Anika told Carlos about the contest, Jeff's accusations, and finally losing to Tasha in fragrances despite all the fuss. She felt relieved, being able to talk to someone who understood.

"Cecilia is loco," Carlos said.

Anika laughed. "I agree, she is crazy."

"I'm not giving up. I've already texted Keira to meet

with her soon about this mess. I don't think you should give up either. I'm not sure how Cecilia can ban you from working with me."

"I don't know what to do. It does seem like she's trying to sabotage your work." Anika lifted one shoulder and let it fall. "I knew it was a temp job coming into this but I hoped that it might turn into something more. I don't know what I'll do." She resisted the urge to cry on Carlos's shoulder. He had been kind to listen to her and she really needed to get back to work before she ended up wrapped in his arms again. "I should probably go. It's so busy out there."

"Try not to worry," Carlos said. "Why don't you take the next couple days off from working with me? We'll steer clear of Cecilia." He squeezed her hand. "I know things are going to work out for Christmas. This time of year there are always a lot of miracles."

Anika shook her head. "I don't need miracles. There are lots of other people hurting much worse than me and Megan." The words were flat, but Anika didn't have the energy to infuse cheerfulness into her lie.

Carlos frowned. "We all need miracles." He let his fingers graze softly over her cheek. "I'll see you later?"

Anika nodded. They walked out of the lounge together and Carlos headed back to the soda fountain. On her way to the women's department, Anika walked over to the children's department and stood in front of the dollhouse on display. The floor model would be discounted by an extra fifteen percent but she'd have to wait until Christmas Eve to buy it. She'd looked up how to make dollhouses on Pinterest out of cardboard boxes, decorative papers, and all kinds of time-consuming projects but she didn't think her attempt would turn out nearly as cute. She chewed on her bottom lip. The extra money she would have made working with Carlos seemed to hang in the air, taunting her. It was a long shot anyway. She'd probably have to make do with something home-made. Megan was such a sweetheart, she'd love a dollhouse made out of cardboard just as much.

"Oh, well. It was a nice dream anyway." Anika touched the edge of the boxes lined up under the display. An iron weight shackled to her heart and pulled everything down. She found it hard to smile for the rest of her shift.

CHAPTER 15

ANIKA ENDED UP WORKING AN EXTRA shift on Saturday, and the store was so busy all she could do was wave at Carlos when he walked by with more building supplies for the soda fountain. They both kept their distance so that Cecilia wouldn't have any proof of flirting. In spite of the Christmas music, shoppers, and wrapping paper that created a warm holiday atmosphere, Anika felt an empty space inside. She missed being with Carlos. That thought stunned her, and frightened her because even though she tried to turn off the yearning for the handsome Puerto Rican with a delicious accent, it grew stronger every day.

Near the end of her shift, Carlos found her hanging up evening wear that would be perfect for Christmas parties and dances, like the Candy Cane Twist.

"Are you picking out your dress for the dance?" he asked.

Anika whirled around and bumped into him. "Don't sneak up on me like that," she whispered, smiling broadly so that he would know she really was fine with him sneaking up on her.

Carlos put a hand on her back and leaned closer. "I have a little good news."

Anika stared at his lips and blinked. "What?"

"Rumor is that Cecilia left for downtown New York today. She won't be back until next week."

"Really?" Anika hugged Carlos and sighed in relief. He'd just released the valve on the mounting pressure that had been building since her meeting with Cecilia. "Maybe I'll have my job for a little while longer."

"I really could use some help on the soda fountain tonight," Carlos whispered in her ear, his arms gently holding her to his chest. For some reason his husky whisper ignited a flame in her middle. Anika tipped her head back. She wanted to kiss him. He looked down at her, one of his thick black eyebrows quirking up in the middle. "I also want to take you on another date."

The bells in the store rung several times in a row as shoppers exited reminding Anika that she was flirting at work. She stepped back from Carlos, but kept her hand on his arm. "But what about Cecilia? She said I couldn't work with you anymore."

"I've thought about it and until I hear back from

Keira I'm going with my gut." Carlos looked in the direction of the soda fountain. "I'll make sure you're paid one way or another."

Anika bit her lip. She didn't want to risk Carlos's job. It wasn't worth getting them both in trouble either. Carlos took her hand in his and tingles shot up her arm. She wanted to be with him. She waited for warning bells to sound after that thought but there were none. Her heart pounded and she squeezed his hand. "I can't tonight. Let's wait until you hear back from Keira and I'll plan on helping you Monday."

Carlos nodded. "Okay, but I want to spend some time with you and Megan. Would you like to go to church with me tomorrow?"

The way he spoke those words with his rolling Spanish accent made Anika weak in more places than her knees, but church? Anika hadn't been to church in a long time, mostly because Jimmy always went to church. Even though she knew that church was for every kind of person and every kind of sin, it didn't seem possible that grace should be offered to someone like Jimmy. Carlos waited for her answer and the silence was nearing awkward. Anika decided to be truthful. "I haven't been to church in a long time. Where do you go?"

"There's a nice old church that rotates through different pastors. Pastor Louis is my favorite and he's preaching tomorrow." There was no judgement in Carlos's eyes. He genuinely wanted her to come.

Anika thought about her meager wardrobe. She didn't own any dresses, but her simple black skirt with a nice blouse would probably work. She sucked in a breath when she remembered that Megan didn't have a dress either. She started to shake her head and Carlos's face fell. "I— uh, I'm thinking about it," she said before Carlos crumpled before her.

He brightened and tucked a strand of hair behind her ear. "Services during the holidays are always great, and they have a potluck tomorrow so you wouldn't have to cook because I'm bringing white chicken chili."

At the mention of holiday services, Anika's thoughts headed down the path toward bah humbug! But when Carlos said there would be a potluck, he got her attention. Megan would love the chance to eat all sorts of food, and Anika's persistent stomach wouldn't complain either. Maybe there was something, a skirt or nicer pants that she could make work for Megan. "What time does church start?"

Carlos grinned. "Can I please pick you up at ten-thirty? Service starts at eleven and we want to get a good seat."

He was breaking down all her barriers tonight, but Anika concentrated on the warmth of his hand in hers. "Sure, let me give you my address."

CARLOS'S STOMACH jumped every time he thought about Anika, but the sensation just made him more excited to pick her and Megan up for church. He had seen the battle going on in Anika's head and immediately connected the dots. Church was probably one more thing that her stupid ex had ruined for her. He prayed for Pastor Louis that his message would be able to penetrate Anika's heart. She was a beautiful woman who had probably once had a vibrant, caring spirit until the man she trusted broke her. Carlos wanted to repair that damage, to have a chance to build a new foundation of hope within Anika, if she'd give him the chance.

He dressed carefully in a forest green button up shirt and silver tie complete with the only dress jacket he owned. Last night he'd been so excited that he even shined his shoes at midnight. His nerves buzzed with a positive energy as he pulled into Anika's parking lot. He was making great strides in their relationship because she trusted him enough to allow him to see where she lived. Just as he'd thought, the apartments weren't far from Eddie's Thrift shop and a line of decrepit stores like the pawn shop, dollar store, and a run-down looking Mexican restaurant. Carlos zipped up his coat and hurried through the freezing temps, climbing icy concrete steps to Anika's second floor apartment.

He knocked on the door and less than a minute later, it opened.

"Good morning," Anika said. She looked lovely in a

black skirt and cream colored blouse with a red beaded necklace.

"Hi, Carlos." Megan squeezed around her mother. "I look pretty!" She twirled and her pink skirt flared up around blue leggings that had a hole in one knee.

"Hello, I'm here to pick up two beautiful ladies," Carlos said and then he lowered his voice to a stage-whisper, "They didn't tell me that you would be this pretty though."

Megan giggled and Anika smiled. They grabbed their coats and Carlos reached out his hands, taking one on each side down the stairs. "Thanks for coming," he said.

"Thanks for the invite. Megan is so excited to go to church." Anika said it like she was confused at Megan's excitement.

Carlos tucked them into his truck and turned the heater up. "I'll never get used to this cold, I guess."

"This? This is nothing?" Anika infused a heavy New Yorker twang to her words. "You should see it when it really snows."

They all laughed and the merry mood carried them through the nervous jitters he sensed in Anika when they walked into the church. The stained glass windows flanking the choir seats sent rainbows of lights on the pews. Carlos noticed Anika studying the trees and flowers twisting through the different colored panes of glass reaching toward the empty tomb where Jesus stood. It was his favorite part of this church. They had arrived early enough to sit closer to the front and within five minutes the chapel had started to fill. Anika sat quietly for a few minutes, murmuring answers to Megan's questions and Carlos hoped she could feel the peace in this old building.

When Pastor Louis stood, Carlos took Anika's hand in his with a gentle squeeze.

"There are many sermons that I could give this time of year about Christ's birth, but I felt impressed to share with you a message regarding the hope that the Savior's birth brought to our world. The hope that it still can bring to each of our hearts."

The congregation quieted and the sun shifted beyond the stained glass windows, sending new rays of light through the chapel. Pastor Louis continued, "In Mark we read that wise men traveled from afar seeking the baby Jesus. I ask you today, have we learned from the wise men? They sought out the Savior because they had hope in prophecies that were thousands of years old. They studied, they worked, and then they traveled incredible distances all with a hope that they would see the newborn King.

"We are on a similar journey in this life, one that requires us to hope in the goodness of the Lord, and in the goodness of all who sojourn here on earth. Sometimes that goodness may seem lost when we are hurt by those not following Jesus and by those who profess to follow Him, but we should never give up on the great gift given to us by a baby's birth. In a lowly manger, in circumstances more poor and simple than most of us can imagine, Jesus Christ came to offer us a gift. How could anyone think that an infant born in these circumstances was a gift?

"The birth of the Savior was a gift because He offered hope to everyone, to all mankind no matter what their station in life was, no matter their race or nationality. He loved everyone, sinner and saint, and His life was the perfect example, the perfect hope for each of us."

The pastor's words sent a thrill through Carlos. They were meaningful to him, but it was as if he was speaking directly to Anika. He wondered if she felt the message radiating through her, the way that he did. She looked over at him, her eyes luminous and his heart seemed to reach toward her. There was so much love for her in that instant. He reached his arm around her and pulled her close to his side, his fingers grazed the top of Megan's head and the little girl smiled over at him. He wanted this— this possibility right next to him. Carlos knew what he wanted for Christmas. He wanted Anika and Megan to feel hope again, not to be afraid of life, but to have joy in the possibilities. And the next thought sent a shock wave through his body. He wanted them in his life.

CHAPTER 16

SITTING SO NEAR TO CARLOS WITH the pastor's words echoing in her heart, Anika felt the faint stirrings of something that she hadn't in years— hope. Sure she had hoped for the money to pay for Megan's doll house. This was different. This was deeper. The type of feeling that resonated in a person's soul, so overwhelming that it could chase out years of treading with light steps and encourage her to step boldly out into the world, filled with, of all dangerous things, hope that everything would work out in the end. That the broken path she'd carefully traversed could be so easily left behind and the dust shaken from her shoes. It was scary, dangerous territory that her logical side screamed at her to run from, hide.

With Carlos's arm around her, and the tender way he

brushed the top of Megan's ponytail with his fingers, Anika was taken back to her childhood. A memory that had been hidden resurfaced. Her mother sat next to her in a pew, holding her hand and singing, *Silent Night.* Goosebumps appeared all over her arms and Anika felt a sensation of peace and warmth come over her. Tears clung to her lashes, and she leaned closer to Carlos. He made her feel safe, like she could do impossible things. Sitting in the pew, looking up at the light blooming through the stained glass filled Anika with the embers of hope. The Savior did offer hope to all, and although she didn't trust her own hope yet, she could lean on Carlos's for a while, borrow a bit of it to keep moving forward.

After the service, they crammed into the reception hall added on to the west wing of the church for the potluck. The aromas of baked goods and warm soups made Anika's mouth water. She laughed when she saw Megan's eyes light up at all the food spread across two long tables. Carlos loaded up an extra plate with all kinds of desserts, waggling his eyebrows at Anika. She laughed and joined him at a table with a couple other parishioners. Megan ate almost everything on her plate and asked for more of Carlos's white chicken chili. He seemed to swell with pride at the four-year-old's praise.

"It is really good," Anika said. "I'd love to have your recipe."

Carlos lifted up a finger and tapped his head. "It's in

here, and it changes a little every time I make it. But for you, I'll write it down."

"You are a man of many talents," she said. "You build things, put out fires, and cook."

"Sometimes I cook and then put out fires, though." Carlos touched Anika's arm and a little thrill went through her. "I think you're pretty talented yourself. Look at this pretty little girl you're raising." He tipped his chin toward Megan.

Anika opened her mouth to argue, to deprecate herself as she often did, instead she accepted his compliment. "Thank you." She was still getting used to the fact that Carlos was sincere— his words meant something to her.

She savored each bite of food. It was the most she'd eaten in months. Carlos introduced her to a few people who came over to greet them, and they were all friendly with a curious gleam to their eye as they took in Carlos next to the new woman and her child. Anika felt welcomed and more comfortable in this church next to Carlos than she would have expected. The difference was Carlos. He made her feel at home, like everything would work out, and with an almost silly hope that maybe happily ever after's did exist.

When it was time to go, Anika wished there was a way to spend more time with Carlos, but she didn't want to come on too strong. If her apartment wasn't so embarrassingly shabby, she'd invite him in. Even as the thought flitted through her mind, she dismissed it. Carlos had shown that he accepted her, but it was probably better if she took some time to clear her head in regards to what was happening with her heart.

"I'm so glad you could come today," Carlos said as he walked Anika and Megan to their apartment. "Would you like to go again next week? There isn't a potluck but I'd love to have you over to my place for dinner."

Anika smiled. "I think it's our turn to feed Carlos. What do you think Megan?"

"I like Carlos's food!" Megan jumped up and down.

Carlos chuckled. "I'll see you tomorrow, okay?" He stepped toward Anika and wrapped her in a hug.

She wondered if he could feel her heart beating through the thick material of their coats because it was thumping in time with the thoughts that Anika wanted to kiss him. Carlos hesitated and then brushed a kiss on her cheek. He stepped back and Anika immediately felt the loss of his touch. She craved his warmth and goodness. Before she could think about how much she wanted to stay in his arms, she turned and shoved her key in the lock. She swung the door open and then turned toward Carlos. "Thank you for a wonderful day."

He nodded and patted Megan's head. Anika saw him glance at her lips before he lifted two fingers in a wave. "My pleasure."

The cold air was seeping inside so Anika hurried in and shut the door even though she wanted to be with

Carlos. She raised a hand to her cheek, thinking of his gentle kiss. Was she crazy to want more? Her toes tingled when she thought about how much more she did want. Was it possible that the dreary future she'd anticipated was about to change?

CHAPTER 17

THE NEXT FEW DAYS WERE HECTIC at Kenworth's leaving Anika and Carlos little time for the flirting they'd been accused of. Anika yearned to be near him in a way that should have had alarms going off but she had finally quieted the doubts circling her mind about men— at least one man.

With Cecilia still out of town, Anika helped Carlos with some of the finish work on the soda fountain. The late nights were wearing on her, but the exhaustion was pushed to the edges whenever she was near Carlos. He lit up her insides like a Christmas tree, and Anika wished there was mistletoe hanging from every aisle in Kenworth's. He hadn't kissed her yet, but every time they were together Anika felt an almost magnetic pull toward him.

On Wednesday, Anika arrived at Kenworth's early.

Christmas was next Friday and everyone was scheduled to work more hours until then, doubling up the amount of sales clerks available to help customers.

Halfway through her shift, there was some cheering near the soda fountain. Carlos had told her he'd be testing out the equipment today with Keira. The nervous ball that had been sitting in her stomach, dissolved when she peeked around The Candy Counter and saw the small group serving up the first ice cream soda. Carlos had wanted Anika to be there, but she thought it was better if he did the test on his own, especially because she was working. Cecilia's accusations still hung heavy over Anika. The threat of not having a job beyond Christmas was still a possibility.

After ringing up a sequence of at least twenty customers, she and Jessica finally hit a lull. "Why don't you take your break now, Anika?" Jessica offered. "I'm going to run and put away some of these items." She tugged on a rolling rack of clothes and headed to the back of the women's department.

Anika glanced at her watch. It was almost seven and she'd been standing in the same spot for three hours. Her legs and feet ached and her stomach complained about its neglect. "I will, but let me know if you get in a bind," she called after Jessica.

Anika stepped around the cash register just as Carlos rounded the corner grinning like he'd just opened his Christmas presents early.

"I have the best news ever," Carlos said. "Come over here." He tugged on her hand, leading her toward the Hope Tree.

"I'm definitely in need of good news," Anika muttered. "Christmas is killing my feet."

Carlos looked down at her feet, and then lifted his face to hers, his smile brighter than ever. Anika raised an eyebrow. "Hmm, this must be really good news."

It didn't seem possible, but Carlos's smile widened. "Cecilia quit!"

"What? Like she's leaving Kenworth's?" Anika held onto Carlos's arms to steady herself.

"Like she already left. Keira just told me that she abandoned them." Carlos squeezed her arms gently.

"That's weird. Why would she do that? I mean, I'm glad, but it doesn't make sense."

"I guess this store has too much Christmas spirit for the Grinch," Carlos said. "I heard something about a better offer in downtown New York. I'm not crying about it though because Keira loved what I've done with the soda fountain and wants me to start on some new projects in the store after Christmas."

"That is the best news I've heard in weeks." Anika could hardly believe that Cecilia was really gone. A weight toppled off her shoulders. There might be a chance for her to continue working at Kenworth's.

"Oh, I think I can top that news," Carlos said. "See, I talked to Keira about how crazy Cecilia has been acting and how she threatened you. Keira said that you aren't going anywhere and she gave me permission to share the good news that they want to hire you on full-time."

Anika leaned back and blinked. It couldn't be. Good things like this didn't happen to her. "It's true?"

Carlos smiled. "Definitely."

She threw her arms around his neck. "Thank you. I can't believe it." She pulled back so she could look in his eyes. "This means everything to me."

"And you mean everything to me," he murmured. He glanced at her lips and tipped his head, slowly coming closer. Anika met him halfway, her lips like a spark of light between them. And then they were kissing and Anika felt her entire body fill with warmth. Carlos put his arms around her waist and pulled her closer, his fingertips leaving little trails of fire along her back.

Her toes tingled and she touched the curls at the nape of his neck with her fingertips. His mouth moved against hers, gentle yet passionate kisses sending fireworks bursting in her chest. She kissed him again and then remembered that they were standing in the middle of the women's department. She took one small step back and bumped into the edge of the Christmas tree. Carlos grabbed the tree before it could tip and then steadied Anika.

"I thought you said you were going to keep your distance the next time you saw me near a Christmas tree." Anika touched the rough stubble on his cheek.

Carlos turned and kissed the palm of her hand. "Hmm, I think maybe you misunderstood."

"Thanks for watching out for me, Carlos." Anika meant what she said. From the first day they'd met, Carlos had been rescuing her little by little. She hadn't wanted to admit it, but she needed rescuing. She leaned in and brushed his lips with hers, the movement sending sparks through her body. Carlos pulled her toward him and kissed her gently. She definitely wanted to stay right there in his arms. His mouth moved against hers with more intensity. She loved the way he held her carefully, but with a strength that said he didn't want to let her go.

"Anika, I love you," he murmured against her cheek.

Her heart thrummed wildly in her chest, a thread of worry blooming next to each heartbeat. Carlos loved her. Jimmy used to tell her he loved her all the time. She'd stopped saying it back to him after the first time he'd hit her. She shoved that thought from her mind. Carlos wasn't Jimmy. Carlos really did love her, he'd shown her that since the first day they'd met. She kissed his mouth again and snuggled in deeper, feeling the pounding of his heart against her chest.

His words hung in the air and Anika tasted them in his kiss. She wanted to say them back, but she was afraid of what might happen to her when she did. It was like tumbling down a dark hole, not knowing where the bottom might be or how she'd land. She wanted to take that leap, but her rational side kept a firm grip on her emotions.

She pulled back and studied Carlos. His dark eyes were full of so much love that she felt a part of her armor breaking away. She tightened her hold around his neck and rested her head against him. "Thank you," she whispered.

LATER THAT NIGHT, Carlos relived every second of that amazing kiss with Anika. His stomach clenched when he thought about how he'd told her he loved her. He wanted to feel stupid over it, but at the same time he couldn't because he knew it was true. He loved Anika, and Megan, and he wanted them in his life. Anika hadn't said the words back, but he was pretty sure she was thinking about it. Her rough past had sealed those words inside and one day he'd break through all her barriers and she would tell him she loved him. He had to believe that because he wasn't going to give up on her, no matter how tough things were.

He sanded another small piece of the dollhouse he was building for Megan. The frame was sturdy and the furniture was simple, but she would love it. The work with the soda fountain was complete and he'd use the extra time to finish his present for Megan. The little girl talked about her Christmas dollhouse nonstop and he'd seen Anika looking at one on display in Kenworth's that he was pretty sure was out of her budget.

He still needed to work on Anika's gift. He was carving a Christmas tree ornament that was in the shape of a Christmas tree. He knew that Anika would understand the significance of the tree, patterned after the Hope tree at Kenworth's where they'd first met, first kissed, and where he hoped to continue to build a future with Anika.

When he'd checked with the Ladies League Christmas council last week, they said that everything was taken care of for Anika and Megan. It was a relief that they would get the things they needed this winter. He had wanted to do more, to give more to her personally, but with Anika's pride and fragile heart, that would be treading in dangerous territory.

He adjusted another part of the dollhouse frame. If everything went well, he'd be able to deliver the gift on Saturday and ease Anika's worries over fulfilling her daughter's Christmas wishes.

THE THURSDAY BEFORE THE CANDY cane twist, Anika came in to work early to cover for Jessica. The store was flooded with holiday shoppers and they all bustled about spending lots of money on gifts. It was as though everyone in Echo Ridge could hear the ticking of the clock counting down to Christmas Eve. To Anika it sounded akin to a death knell — the death of her young daughter's dreams. Maybe she shouldn't put so much emphasis on fulfilling Megan's wish list, but as a child, Anika remembered very little of happy Christmases. She remembered feeling cold, hungry, and wearing shoes that seemed to suck in all the ice and snow to numb her little feet. At least she had provided better for Megan in that respect.

The competition for the store credit would most likely go to the children's department. Tayton had been updating them on sales, encouraging them to work hard on their goals, but Anika knew it was better not to hope for something that wasn't going to happen. She'd all but given up on the idea of a dollhouse for Megan. Instead, she'd buy her a new doll and together, they'd play in their apartment, allowing imagination to create a huge doll house among couch cushions and blankets.

Anika rolled her shoulders back and decided to be grateful for the things she did have— a drafty apartment, a temporary job, Megan, and possibly an incredibly fine man named Carlos. Her smile finally turned genuine when she thought of Carlos. It still seemed risky to consider dating him, and the future that might entail but he was changing her as if he'd cleaned the lens she used to view the world. Carlos had also grown up with very little and still struggled, working several jobs to attain his dream yet he kept a positive attitude. That's what she needed, a little dose of Carlos. Anika hummed along to "Walking in a Winter Wonderland" as she put away winter items and mounds of clothing.

After she finished hanging up all the clothes from the dressing rooms, Anika took over for Jessica at the cash register.

"Do you have a dress for the dance?" Jessica asked.

"Not yet. I might just have to wear my black skirt." Anika twisted her hands together. The thought of the dance had been dogging her ever since she went to church and noticed the beautiful dresses several of the women wore. They weren't flaunting their clothing, but Anika had been looking. Her skirt was fine for church but she would be underdressed for the dance. At least she would match Megan— who didn't have a nice dress either.

"Oh, no. That won't do," Jessica said. "This is your first dance with Carlos. We have to make you shine. There's a red dress over in petites that's marked down. It has a fitted bodice with a side seam zipper. You ought to try it on."

"Jessica, I probably can't afford it. I just don't have any extra money right now." Anika turned away so her manager wouldn't see the redness creeping into her cheeks.

Jessica frowned and tapped the side of her cheek. "I'm sure something will work out. I'm not going to give up, so you can't either! What would it hurt to just try it on?"

Anika remembered the hope she'd felt on Sunday. It would take work to trust that feeling, but she wanted to put herself out there to see if it would grow. She swallowed and nodded. "Okay, I'll see if I have a minute to try it on."

"How about now?" Jessica asked. "I'll wait here for a few minutes and you can go take a peek. It's hanging on the back side of the clearance rack."

Anika sighed. It was better to oblige Jessica than try to win a fashion fight. "I'll hurry."

The clearance rack was stuffed with clothes, many of them from last season. Anika pushed aside some ugly green and orange dresses and gasped when the red dress came into view. The bodice shimmered with a line of crystal beading that fell in a slant toward the flared skirt. Anika ran her hands over the fabric— a blend of rayon and probably polyester. It hung beautifully, shining like a Christmas ornament.

She held the dress up to her as she walked into the dressing room and gazed in the mirror. Even without trying it on, she could tell it was perfect. A bell chimed somewhere in the store— a customer needing assistance — and Anika snapped out of her reverie. She turned the dress around and dug inside for the price tag. Another gasp, this one with no delight, escaped her lips. The regular price of the dress was eighty-nine dollars and it had been marked down to thirty-nine, definitely a can't-miss deal. Anika's shoulders slumped, and she walked back to the racks and hung up the dress. Even with her twenty percent employee discount, the dress would be about thirty-two dollars with tax and she didn't have that much money. She trailed her fingers along the beading, and with a sigh walked back to the cash register.

Before she rounded the corner she pasted a smile on her face. "You're right. That dress is absolutely gorgeous. It will be perfect."

Jessica clapped her hands. "I knew it! I can't wait to see you in it. Okay, gotta run." She left in a rush of curls and a lingering scent of vanilla and peppermint. She didn't really understand what Anika meant when she said she didn't have enough money. Most people thought that meant you couldn't go on vacation or buy those three-hundred-dollar pair of jeans. Most people could come up with thirty-two dollars to buy a discount dress.

Anika leaned against the counter for a minute, trying to shake the fog of doubts shrouding her. Who was she kidding? Dating Carlos was a bad idea. She couldn't even afford a discounted dress to wear to the dance. Carlos had said he didn't mind what she wore, but when they got there and everyone, especially the Ice Money, was dressed in their furs and sequins, he'd see her for the washed-up wannabe she really was. Tears pricked the corner of her eyes and she blinked, swiping a hand across her eyes angrily. It was no use pretending. She hated Christmas and a good attitude couldn't change the fact that she was two steps away from poverty. Anika shrugged. The grandfather clock was busy chiming out the seventh hour. It was nearly rush hour at the store. She looked up and saw a line forming at her cash register. Thankfully, she could lose herself in her work instead of wallowing in her worries.

"Did you find everything you needed tonight?" she asked the first woman, infusing a false cheerfulness into her voice.

"Yes, lots of great gifts," the young woman said as she

piled her merchandise on the counter. "I just love Kenworth's at Christmas time."

Anika nodded, trying to swallow the lump in her throat that was lodged like a piece of fruitcake leftover from the holidays. She worked that way for another hour, trying to breathe around the pressure weighing down on her that had everything to do with Christmas.

"I'm so glad someone told me about this lovely Christmas tree," a sweet voice interrupted Anika's miserable thoughts.

She looked up to meet the welcoming smile of an elderly woman. The woman adjusted a strand of her beautifully styled silver-white hair. Her nails were manicured with tiny red gems set in painted holly berries. She put her purse on the counter and it was all Anika could do to resist reaching out to touch the supple leather in a deep shade of burgundy. The woman smiled brightly. "The Hope Tree is such a wonderful idea. I love the thoughts of being able to help people right here in our own community. I don't know why but it just means more to me to buy something for people in Echo Ridge rather than to give a few dollars to some huge national charity. This just feels more like what an old-fashioned Christmas is all about."

Anika nodded as the woman babbled on. It was hard not to catch a bit of her Christmas spirit. If Mrs. Claus herself were to help Santa and the elves with shopping,

Anika thought that maybe she would look a lot like this woman.

Her blue eyes sparkled behind rimless glasses. "Isn't this dress exquisite?" She lifted up the red dress Anika was supposed to wear to the Candy Cane Twist.

Anika swallowed. "I love it." At least she was telling the truth.

"It seemed like this dress was just calling me to buy it, so I hunted around and look what I found hanging on the Hope Tree." She lifted up a cream colored card and dangled it in front of Anika's nose.

Anika opened the card and read,

Woman's Evening dress, size 4

Thank you for your support of The Hope Tree and Echo Ridge.

Merry Christmas from Kenworth's!

Well, at least her dress was going to someone for a good cause. Anika pulled out a dress box, folded it and tucked in a sheet of tissue paper. "Here, I'll snip the price off the tag and wrap it up for you."

"Wonderful," Mrs. Claus said. "And I have another one here." She handed Anika a Christmas dress that looked like it was made for Megan and a pair of jeans with pink stitching and rhinestones on the pockets. "Here's the tag that goes with them."

Anika flipped open each of the cards and read them. Her heart stuttered when she read:

Girl's dress, Age 4, Size 4T

Girl's pants, Age 4, Size 4T

She looked up, studying Mrs. Claus. It was a strange coincidence that she was purchasing items from the Hope Tree that were exactly what Anika would have wanted for Christmas if she could choose.

"What is it dear? Did I get the wrong size?"

"Uh— no, these are great," Anika stammered. "I just was thinking these jeans would be perfect for my little girl." She didn't add that the price tag of twenty-one dollars meant Megan would never have a pair like those. They shopped at thrift stores and thankfully there were many good pieces to find— Ice Money castoffs. Anika smoothed a hand over her black slacks. She'd picked them up on a special sale at the thrift store for five dollars.

"I bet she's a little doll," the woman said. "With a darling mother working so hard to make her Christmas special. She's lucky."

Anika paused, holding the dress in midair, and murmured, "Thank you." Maybe she really was Mrs. Claus. With one interchange, she'd pegged Anika's situation exactly.

Anika wrapped up the gifts and rang up the rest of the items Mrs. Claus had stacked on the counter. Normally, she'd be thinking all kinds of nasty thoughts about the woman purchasing items for the Hope Tree recipients, but her sparkling eyes and cheerful laugh stole the meanness right out of Anika.

"Merry Christmas from Kenworth's," Anika said automatically.

The woman tilted her head. "Merry Christmas to you."

Anika found herself reliving the conversation with the Mrs. Claus look-alike for the rest of the evening. Something about the coincidence made her wonder, but she worked through her thoughts until closing time. She missed working with Carlos and couldn't wait to see him tomorrow. She put a finger to her lips, wishing he was here now to kiss away the nagging worries about Christmas.

CHAPTER 19

FRIDAY MORNING, MEGAN WAS BUSY coloring a picture for Santa— the fridge was covered in her artwork— and singing to herself while Anika wrote a check for another medical payment.

Right now she could really use that quarter. As much as she despised Christmas, she was trying to come up with some way to make it special for Megan. If her idea didn't work then all the hard work to prove to herself that they weren't trash would go unnoticed when Santa passed by their house on Christmas Eve. The only thing worse than getting a lump of coal for Christmas is getting nothing— nothing at all.

The numbers on the bills blurred, and Anika sucked in a breath reminding herself to stay strong. The heating bill was ten dollars more than she'd planned on and the city utilities had an extra fee for updating the garbage dumpsters. She had scrounged up the last of her change and even borrowed two dollars from Megan's piggy bank to pay the bills. Her eyes strayed to the cupboard where she knew there was one box of Tuna Helper ready to bake with the last can of tuna fish. She pulled out another bill and wondered if there was anything she could pawn to get some extra money. Anika sighed. There was nothing. Maybe they were trash— she didn't even own anything worth more than a trip to the junk yard.

When the doorbell rang Anika looked up from the pile of bills, insurance statements, and small wad of money she was trying to make sense of. Maybe it was Carlos stopping by to say hello and rescue her from the drudgery of trying to make a dollar stretch farther than pulled taffy. The thought made her pause because whenever she heard a knock, her first thoughts used to be of Jimmy. Even though she'd moved to Echo Ridge, not leaving a trace of her past to follow her, she still worried that he would find them someday. But Carlos was slowly erasing her fears.

"Keep coloring, Meggie. Mommy will answer the door." Anika walked toward the door and peered through the peephole. She didn't recognize the two women standing outside, but they looked harmless so she opened the door.

"Anika Fletcher?" the woman with short brown hair asked.

"Yes, that's me."

"Oh, good. Merry Christmas, Anika!" The other woman with a bright red dress coat and dangly silver bell earrings smiled broadly. She stepped aside and that's when Anika noticed the box full of wrapped gifts on her doorstep.

"What?" Anika glanced behind her. Too late, Megan was already at her heels bouncing over the Christmas greetings.

"Who is it Mommy? Hi, I'm Megan," she announced.

Before Anika could speak, a man and two young girls rounded the corner carrying more Christmas gifts.

"I have a present for the little girl!" A girl about Megan's age jumped up and down with a golden bell tinkling in her hand.

"Mine first," a little voice called out belonging to another little girl pushing her way around her father's leg.

The father grinned, lifting a huge box filled with wrapped Christmas presents. "May I put this inside?"

Anika didn't know what to say. She nodded in confusion as he hauled the box in and set it in the living room. "I'll be right back," he said and winked.

"Look, look we have more." One of the little girls squealed as the woman with the dangly earrings lifted another box and carried it into the apartment.

"But how——" She started to ask and her lip trembled.

"It's Christmas, that's how. Miracles happen every day and twice a day around Christmas." The woman reached her arms toward Anika in a hug. "I hope that you and your daughter have a wonderful Christmas. This is for you to open after we leave." She handed Anika a beautiful gold envelope.

She heard more squeals of delight as someone called out, "Ho, ho ho!" The little girls danced around their father carrying in a beautiful Christmas tree and Megan laughed with joy. It was small, but the perfect size for their little apartment. He handed Anika a sack full of ornaments and quickly fastened the tree into the stand.

"I can't believe it," Anika mumbled. "How did you know?"

"Daddy says we're Christmas angels," one of the little girls said.

"You must be," she said. "Thank you so much."

"Merry Christmas," the man said and held out his hand. Anika shook it and gave him a watery smile.

The group was all smiles as they left the apartment. Anika stared at the beautiful Christmas tree with boxes of presents underneath.

"Mommy, can we open this one?" Megan danced around with a present in her hands.

"No, honey, we have to wait until—" Anika stopped, staring at the box with gold and green wrapping paper and a red bow. The box that she had wrapped last night at Kenworth's. It couldn't be the same one. "Here, let me look at that." She took the box from Megan who protested for a moment before running back to the tree to pull out another present.

Anika's hand shook as she lifted the cream-colored card that read,

Merry Christmas from the Hope Tree at Kenworth's!
Celebrate Echo Ridge!

The woman who looked just like Mrs. Claus came to mind. How did the Hope Tree get her and Megan's information? Anika shook her head and lifted the edge of the wrapping paper, careful not to tear it. She slid her finger along the tape and uncovered the Kenworth's box. She held her breath as she opened the lid. Under the layer of tissue paper was the red dress.

"No," Anika whispered because everything suddenly made sense. She was pretty sure how her name had ended up on that tree. She clenched her fists, crinkling the tissue paper. Her face burned and hot tears coursed down her cheeks. All this time, Carlos was getting to know her so that he could give the information to the Christmas Council. The kiss, had that been part of his ruse? Come to think of it, the family looked familiar, were they part of the congregation at the church? She was a charity case. Anika wiped her face on her sleeve and watched Megan flitting around the Christmas tree, touching the presents and giggling. Anika knew she should be happy, but her heart beat askew in her chest, every beat flaring the pain coursing through her body. Carlos was a good man, but she was his Christmas project, nothing more.

CHAPTER 20

CARLOS WALKED UP THE STEPS to Anika's apartment balancing the giant wrapped box. He couldn't wipe the grin off his face. He'd passed the group of people in the parking lot, smiling and talking about delivering their gifts. Someone else had just received a wonderful expression of love from the community. When he'd talked with the Christmas council, they shared that the plan was to get most of the gifts to recipients a week before Christmas to relieve any stress and worry about making the holiday bright.

He'd sped on the way over, slowing down around the icy patches on the roads because he was so excited to deliver his gift. He also wanted Anika to relax and enjoy the rest of the holiday season, knowing that everything was taken care of— that Megan's wish for Santa would come true.

The doll house had taken more time than he'd antici-pated but it had been so energizing to work on it, imag-ining the smile on Megan's face when she saw it. He only wished he could be there with her and Anika Christmas morning. The thought made his heart speed up. He wanted to be with Anika and Megan— he loved them both. Carlos set the box down carefully and knocked on the door, hoping his own Christmas miracle could come to pass.

Anika opened the door, her eyes red and her face splotchy from crying. "What do you want?"

Carlos's smile fell at the venom in her voice. He scrambled to assess the situation because something must have gone wrong. "I— uh, brought a special Christmas gift for Megan. I don't have yours finished yet, but I wanted you to know that I made this so that you wouldn't have to stress anymore." He picked up the box and moved to walk inside but Anika didn't open the door wider. "Anika?"

"Well, I guess you can check us off your list early then, right?" she spat.

Carlos looked over her shoulder and saw Megan dancing around a little Christmas tree. There was a pile of ornaments on the kitchen table. "Megan looks happy. And you got a tree." He tried a smile again. "Is there something wrong?"

"Oh, everything is just peachy," Anika said. "Espe-cially since you don't seem surprised at all to see a

Christmas tree in my living room with lots of presents underneath it."

He lifted his eyebrows. "Why would anyone be surprised to see a Christmas tree in someone's house in December?"

"With presents," she said.

Carlos nodded slowly. "Yes, with presents. Still not a surprise for anyone."

"Don't play dumb with me," Anika said. "I know it was you. The Hope Tree? Really, Carlos? Don't you think it's just a tiny bit humiliating even for someone like me who doesn't have any pride left— to wrap her own Christmas present?"

Carlos stepped back. Something had definitely gone terribly wrong. Anika wasn't happy at all. She was angry, and something else. He looked at her closer, listening to her words. She was ashamed. "Wait, what do you mean The Hope Tree?"

"Some people just stopped by here with gifts that were purchased from Kenworth's." Anika turned and pointed to an unwrapped gift on the table. "I wrapped that gift last night and heard the woman talking about what a neat program The Hope Tree was for those less fortunate." She turned to Carlos and folded her arms. "Nice move, Carlos, having someone buy me a dress so that I could go to the dance with you. I guess if I look around, I'll probably find the Christmas dress I wrapped for a four-year-old girl last night too, right?"

Carlos opened his mouth. "I— Anika, I came to give you a gift that I made for Megan. It's a dollhouse," he whispered. "I've been working on it for weeks. I wanted to surprise you but I don't know what's going on."

Anika stopped talking, folded her arms over her chest, and glared. Her eyes flitted to the large box he was holding.

"Please. Can I just put this under the tree?" Carlos didn't want to force his way into the apartment, but there was no way he would leave before delivering his gift. Megan deserved it, even if Anika was freaking out over something he couldn't piece together. Anika sniffed and pulled the door open. He set the box down carefully against the wall behind the tree.

"Hi, Megan. Are you excited for Christmas?"

Megan bounced up and down and clapped her hands. "Santa's helpers brought our presents early so that I could look at them!"

The sheer joy on her face warmed Carlos down to his toes. He touched one of the gift tags on the present and it opened revealing a Merry Christmas message from Kenworth's. He pulled his fingers back as if he'd been burned. Anika's words fell into place in his head. All of the gifts under the tree had been purchased at Kenworth's from the very Hope Tree she had set up and decorated. He blinked, realizing that somehow it was his fault. But then Megan caressed the shiny gold wrapping paper on one of the gifts and giggled. Maybe there was a way to fix the situation. If he could explain that it was a misunderstanding.

Carlos turned and smiled at Anika, but her frown wouldn't budge. "You can leave now." Her voice was flat.

He stood and walked to Anika. Explaining that he turned their names into the Christmas council would probably make things worse instead of better. "I'm trying to understand why you're so angry, I really am. But all I can see is Megan glowing with happiness and it doesn't seem like a bad thing to me that someone helped you out for Christmas."

"I didn't ask for help. We're doing just fine on our own."

"No, you're not doing just fine," Carlos said, struggling to keep his voice even. "You're struggling. You're working too hard and someone decided to give you a hand up. It's okay to accept help, especially when it's given with love."

Anika turned and walked to the door. "Goodbye Carlos. I don't want to see you again."

Carlos's chest constricted. How could she be so angry? Carlos wasn't even sure if these gifts were because of him. What if someone else had turned in her name too? "Anika, please don't do this."

"I don't want to be your charity case. I'm tired of being treated like trash." She opened the door and stepped to the side.

"I never treated you like trash," Carlos said. His

shoulders slumped. "Can't you see that the people in Echo Ridge are reaching out to each other? I'm sorry that you had to wrap your own present. I'm sure that wasn't planned, but this isn't just about you." He tilted his head toward Megan who had stopped dancing and watched them now with worry wrinkling her forehead.

"Exactly. That's why I have to protect my daughter. Good-bye." She pulled the door open wider and a draft of cold air whooshed inside.

Carlos hung his head and walked through the door. Anika was too angry to reason with, the door slamming shut behind him accentuated that thought. He tromped down the stairs, careful to miss the chunks of ice and snow leftover from the storm.

When he turned in the information on Anika and Megan he'd told the sub for Santa program it needed to find donors separate from the Hope Tree at Kenworth's because she worked there. Someone obviously had lost that message. He groaned and rubbed his forehead. Anika was so angry, he couldn't think of a way to undo this mess. He wished she would let go of her anger at Christmas— that somehow she could find joy in the season. Carlos had grown up in a different environment. There had never been much to spare, but Christmas had always been a wonderful celebration anyway.

He had noticed the beautiful red dress sitting in the box on the table. It would be humiliating to wrap your own present, but if there were no other options for

Christmas why not just accept the gifts? For some reason Anika had decided that he didn't love her, that it was all a charity case. He had to convince her otherwise, but he wasn't sure how to do that. It would definitely take a Christmas miracle.

CHAPTER 21

ANIKA CALLED IN SICK FOR WORK on Saturday. She texted Carlos that she wouldn't be going to the dance or church with him over the weekend. Then she ignored his texts and calls. She holed up in her apartment glaring at the presents every time she walked by.

On Monday she returned to work, swallowing back the tears she wanted to cry when she approached the Hope Tree. She had almost walked past before she noticed that every branch was bare. No tags with sizes and ages hung from the branches. "Jessica, what happened to the Hope Tree?"

"Some woman came in and took every tag that was left and bought stuff from our store to give to them." Jessica polished off the mahogany counter. "You know, she didn't look like she even had that kind of money. Like someone who'd never shopped at our store before."

"Oh." Anika's heart tingled and her throat felt tight. A piece of her cynic's armor figuratively fell to the ground.

"Hey, we missed you at the dance," Jessica said. "That is such a bummer you were sick. I noticed that red dress was gone and it just hurt right here to not see you dancing in it with Carlos." Jessica covered her chest.

Anika sighed. "I've been working too hard."

"You look more than tired. Are you sure you're okay?"

Anika nodded. "I'll check on the displays." She turned before Jessica could see the tears threatening to fall from her lashes.

CARLOS TIGHTENED the screws in the new cabinets he'd just installed in his bathroom. With the extra money from the soda fountain job, he'd finally be able to finish the master bath— a huge selling point. Winter hung heavy in the air outside and his thoughts turned to sunny Florida where the rest of his family lived. It would be running away, but he was thinking about selling his house and starting over. If he couldn't have Anika, he didn't want Echo Ridge.

He'd tried calling her but she wouldn't answer. It was almost Christmas, and just a few days ago he thought it was going to be one of the best Christmases ever, spending time with Anika and Megan, dreaming about the future. He'd worked hard on his house so when they came over for Christmas dinner, Anika would be comfortable and maybe see the possibility of a future with him. The home was small but it had three bedrooms — enough for a family. Carlos worked past the despair emanating from his fingertips. There was only one thing he wanted for Christmas, but he was old enough to know that Santa couldn't help him.

"C'MON MEGAN. MOMMY WILL ONLY be a few more minutes and then I'll take you home and you can go right to bed." Anika tugged on Megan's hand and hurried her to the back of the store.

Lila had a family Christmas party to attend so she'd watched Megan until six and then dropped her off at Kenworth's. It wasn't perfect, but it was much better than entertaining a four-year old during a six-hour work shift. Hopefully she could make it through the night without anyone noticing Megan. With Cecilia gone most of her fears had also left, but she still wanted to show Kenworth's that they had made the right choice in keeping her on. Anika's shoulders were tight knots of stress and cords of tension over the fear of having her job threatened again because of her daughter.

"Is Santa coming tonight?" her daughter asked.

"Tomorrow night." Anika tucked a blanket around Megan and her daughter snuggled deeper into the couch. The employee break room wasn't the best place for a child to sleep, but at least she would be out of trouble and Anika could finish her shift.

Anika wouldn't have to lie to Megan about Santa. The gifts from the Hope Tree had saved her Christmas even if it had also destroyed her chance of love with Carlos. A tiny thought nudged the back of her mind, the one that said she didn't understand the true spirit of Christmas, but Anika shoved that thought away angrily. She wanted love, not pity. She needed someone who wanted her family not just because they wanted to save her, but because he really wanted to be with her and her daughter.

She thought of Carlos's house— she'd driven by it last week. It was a small bungalow and the hard work Carlos had put into fixing it up was obvious. A lump of tears tore at the back of her throat. It was almost perfect. Almost.

The store had been busy all day with last-minute Christmas shoppers. The Hope Tree stood beautifully decorated, yet empty without the dozens of cream-colored cards filled with information of people in need. Anika glared at the tree, the anger rising up in the back of her throat as she thought about the kiss she shared with Carlos. He'd told her he loved her and she'd believed him. *Never again*, she silently swore to herself. The lights flickered and the tree suddenly dimmed. A few of the overhead lights sputtered and the bright fluorescent lights in the children's area went out.

That was strange. Anika checked her watch, it was fifteen minutes until closing. She shrugged, somebody was in a hurry to start celebrating their Christmas break. That was fine with her. Kenworth's closed early on Christmas Eve before her shift tomorrow. Anika was looking forward to the time off, even if it meant she wouldn't be earning money. The thought of money brought her back around to the wrapped presents and Christmas tree in her cramped apartment and her blood pressure began to rise. She gritted her teeth and tried to think of something else. The something else was Carlos. She couldn't get him out of her head; his brown eyes, caramel skin, and broad shoulders that could so easily carry anything placed upon them. He was a good guy, just misdirected.

Anika caught a glimpse of herself in the mirror next to the stylish scarves and hats. Maybe the problem did lie within her. Jessica had hinted as kindly as possible that Anika was related to the Grinch. Looking at the deep frown lines on her forehead, and the bags under her eyes was depressing. She turned away and went back to work.

Anika put her hand in the pocket of the soft blue sweater she had pulled on tonight. Her fingers grazed the edge of a paper. She pulled out a gold envelope with her name written on it. Where had that come from? She tried to remember the last time she'd worn the blue sweater. Her throat tightened— it was last week, the day after she had rung up her own red dress for Mrs. Claus. The day that family had delivered her Christmas presents and she'd told Carlos she didn't want to see him anymore. She recalled hanging the sweater in her closet, completely forgetting the Christmas card inside.

Tears came to her eyes and Anika's lip trembled as she opened the flap of the envelope. There was so much hurt in her heart and she knew it was wrong to hold onto the pain. If only there was a way to fix the mess she was in. She gently pulled out a card with silver snowflakes embossed on the front and a holiday greeting. Her thumb rubbed the puffy snow-like felt on the card as she lifted the flap. She gasped when three one-hundred dollar bills fluttered out. She examined the bills— they were real. She folded them into her pocket as she focused on the delicate handwriting filling up the card's interior.

ANIKA,

Hate and cynicism are just like a slow-killing poison. The longer you hold on to your anger and hopelessness the more it permeates your soul. Soon, you are encased with the poison and it distorts your view of the world.

This Christmas and from now on, let hope, peace, joy, and love permeate your soul. Love casteth out all fear. God loves you. These gifts are so you can see the world through His eyes for a small moment—a moment that will change your heart forever if you let Him in.

    Love,

    Your Christmas Angel

ANIKA STARED at the words that struck her soul like a hot knife. Whoever wrote this note didn't just know that she didn't have money for Christmas, they knew her. The script was feminine and the twinkling blue eyes and silver-white hair of Mrs. Claus came to mind. Could she have written the note?

The clock started chiming nine tolls for the store's closing, and Anika quickly tucked the card back into her sweater, her mind churning with thoughts and ideas about how she'd acted toward everyone in the past week leading up to Christmas. Guilt pricked at her conscience, and she almost stopped to reread the card's message. Instead, Anika hurried to the front door to lock up. She was tired and there was no way she was going to play Mrs. Claus and let someone in for one last purchase. She bolted the door and returned to clean out her cash register, tally receipts, and all the other monotonous tasks that had to be completed no matter how exhausted she was. Thankfully, Megan hadn't ventured out from the employee lounge which meant she had fallen asleep.

Anika shouldered a bag full of miscellaneous items that needed to be restocked and walked across the floor toward the men's department. She pulled a tie out of the bag and was about to hang it next to the others when she thought of the way Gentry had treated her. She walked over to his register and dumped the items on the counter with a smug grin. Those items could wait until tomorrow to be restocked.

She'd made it halfway across the store when her nose started to itch with something acrid like the smell of melted plastic. Worried that something might be amiss in the employee lounge, Anika hurried to the back of the store. Just before she reached the main offices, the smoke alarm went off.

Anika bolted at the sound and sprinted into the employee lounge. Megan's blanket hung off one side of the sofa, but her daughter wasn't sleeping next to it. Anika searched the room and when she didn't find Megan, she screamed alongside the wail of the fire alarm. "Megan, Mommy's here! Megan!"

Anika slid around the corner, the overhead sprinklers were on in the children's department and the water was running across the floor. She called for Megan and gulped in a mouthful of black smoke. She coughed as she ran and pulled her shirt up over her nose. Her heart pounded frantically, keeping time to the panic coursing through Anika's veins. She coughed until her eyes streamed with tears. The worst of the smoke was billowing out from the children's section— the place where Megan had delightfully played among the

Christmas displays and drove a pink car along the new shelves Carlos had built.

"Help! Is there anyone in here? My four-year-old is in the store!" Anika yelled. Her cell phone was tucked inside her purse in the closet of the employee lounge. There wasn't time to call for help. If Megan was in the children's section, she could die of smoke inhalation in minutes. Anika grabbed one of the winter scarves she'd seen earlier and tied it around her face. Gulping a breath, she ran into the black smoke billowing up and curling along the ceiling. She couldn't see any flames yet, but the temperature rose as she approached the children's section.

"Megan! Megan! Mommy needs you. We have to get ready for Santa Claus!" Anika stumbled over a display of toys, banged her knee into a table and chair set, and landed on top of some stuffed Christmas bears. She coughed and her eyes burned. Where was Megan? Her daughter was in the store somewhere. Anika thought she heard a shout, but it sounded far away. Her head throbbed and her mouth tasted like black ash. She pulled herself up and headed toward Santa's throne, but Megan wasn't there either. She was about to check in the employee lounge again when she thought she heard music playing. The familiar notes of *Silent Night* filtered through the store and it seemed to be coming from her station in the women's department. Anika tried to run forward, but her legs buckled and she collapsed on the floor. She pulled herself to a crawling position and squinted to make out the display of sweaters and Christmas gifts next to her cash register. Megan had to be there. Anika crawled toward the Christmas melody playing, wondering where the music was coming from.

"Megan," her words came out as a broken whisper etched in smoke. Everything was a blur, the only thing that was clear was the music. Anika's body felt like a cement slab. Her lungs felt like she was breathing glass. She had to find Megan. She crawled toward the sound of *Silent Night* until she could see the Hope Tree flickering ahead.

CHAPTER 23

WHEN THE TEXT CAME FROM the fire department to report to Kenworth's department store at nine-thirty, Carlos panicked. Anika was there closing up. The building was almost a hundred years old. He could see the fire consuming the wood and plaster walls like a hungry dragon. Carlos didn't want to waste time stopping at the fire department for his gear. He texted his buddy, Damon, and asked him to bring it to the store with an urgent message that people could be in danger. It was against protocol and he could get sidelined for it, but all Carlos could think of was Anika.

The sky was heavy with dark clouds and only a few pinpricks of starlight made it through the threatening snowstorm. Carlos sped through town and pulled around back at Kenworth's. He cried out when he saw Anika's red car and drove through the alleyway toward the front of the store.

He sucked in a breath when he saw the #2 fire engine hooking up hoses. Carlos jumped from his pickup and ran to the engine where Damon was manning a hose. Damon saw him coming and thumbed behind him.

"It's in the truck. Dude, you owe me, cuz they said the store is clear."

Carlos shoved past Damon, yelling. "People inside! There are people inside! Anika Fletcher is inside." He stopped just long enough to pull on his turnouts, yank on his helmet, and steal an SCBA, to provide fresh air, from one of the other firefighters before he sprinted for the front doors. He grabbed another firefighter by the arm who was coming out of the building. "I need you to go back in with me. There are people inside." Carlos didn't wait for an answer, just pulled on his fellow firefighter and dashed inside.

Firemen were yelling all kinds of commands as he jumped hoses and shouldered his way into the black smoke belching from the building. He slid the tank's straps over his shoulders and flipped it one, running towards the women's department.

Carlos found Anika on the ground next to a rack of dresses. He sucked in a breath of the fresh air flowing from his mask. The acrid smoke boiled up against the ceiling of Kenworth's. The fire crew was right behind him spraying down the flames erupting all over the children's section. Thank goodness he'd found Anika in time. He lifted her in his arms and carried her out the front of the store. She was unconscious, and he wasn't sure if she was breathing.

A paramedic met him at the front doors with a stretcher. Carlos set Anika down, his mind buzzing with questions. Why hadn't Anika left the store when the alarms sounded? Something wasn't right. And then his skin turned ice cold despite the sweat building up inside his suit.

Megan.

Carlos turned and shouted, "I think this woman's daughter is inside." He pointed at the police officer on scene. "Someone find out if Megan Fletcher is with a sitter. I'm going inside."

He re-entered the store, whispering a silent prayer, "Please God, help me find her." Carlos had to find her. Everything he'd tried to tell Anika about the goodness in life— she'd never believe again if she lost her daughter.

A MAELSTROM of sounds drummed against Anika's ears. There was a whooshing sound, sirens, men hollering, beeps, and clangs everywhere. Her eyes felt like stiff paper maché and her throat felt like she'd swallowed sand. Beyond all the noise she heard music and felt an urgency to open her eyes. She was so tired. If only she could sleep. But there was something about that song. The words came to her mind, *Sleep in heavenly peace.* Anika coughed, and sat bolt upright. "My daughter! Megan is in the store somewhere!"

The EMT froze, her eyes widening. "How old is she?"

"She's four," Anika rasped. "I couldn't find her." She swung her legs over the side of the stretcher and the world tilted.

"Hold on! You can't go anywhere." The EMT steadied her. "My name's Carolyn, and I promise you, those fireman out there are the best bet for finding your daughter." Carolyn grabbed her radio at the same time a fireman poked his head inside the ambulance. "This woman says her daughter is inside the store."

"Carlos is inside looking for her," the fireman answered. "Description?" he looked at Anika.

"Four year old. Dark brown hair, and she was wearing a red Christmas sweater."

"I'm going in." He turned and jogged toward the store.

"I couldn't find her," Anika sobbed. "She wasn't in the back. Not in the children's section."

"Where do you think she could be?" Carolyn asked.

"I work in the women's department so I was going to look there," Anika said. "I must have passed out."

"I'll let them know." Carolyn clicked on her radio and repeated what Anika had told her.

Anika leaned forward, covering her face with her hands, and cried, "Please, Lord. Don't take my baby girl."

CARLOS HEARD the reports coming in on the radio that confirmed Megan was in the store. His stomach went up into his throat when he saw Anika's work station wreathed in smoke. The heat from the back of the store was intense and the fire rumbled somewhere out of sight. There was no sign of Megan around the cash register. Carlos took two steps toward the heat emanating from the children's department and stopped. He scrambled around the cash register and ripped open the cupboard, pawing inside. It was empty. He'd seen Megan dart inside these cupboards to hide and play with her dolls. He pulled open another cupboard stuffed full of hangers. Carlos turned and opened the last cupboard. Megan lay curled up inside, her head resting on a pile of cloth shopping bags. He grabbed hold of her and lifted her from the cupboard.

Megan's eyes fluttered, and opened as Carlos hurried toward the front of the store. She screamed when she saw Carlos. He flinched, but then grinned because she was screaming at his helmet, and screaming meant she was breathing.

"It's okay, Meggie. It's Carlos. I've got you and I'm taking you to your mommy." His voice was muffled, but

Megan stopped and peered at him through the helmet. Then she reached up a hand and rapped on the plexiglass.

"Carlo?" she asked.

Carlos chuckled. "Yep, it's me." He held Megan tight and pushed past the hose vibrating with water. As soon as he was clear of the building, he pulled off his helmet and shouted, "I've got her." He lifted Megan, and a cheer went up. Carlos located the ambulance and hugged Megan to him. "Let's go see your mom."

CHAPTER 24

CHRISTMAS MORNING LOOKED LIKE the sparkling silver card Anika had kept near her since the night of the fire. She'd almost memorized the words and promised herself that she would change her life and Megan's. During her overnight stay in the hospital, she decided that never again would she stomp through life hating Christmas.

Carlos arrived at her apartment just in time for break-fast. Anika's heart fluttered when she opened the door and saw the three white roses he held toward her. "Merry Christmas, Anika."

She pulled Carlos inside and touched his cheek. "Merry Christmas to you." She wrapped her arms around his neck and kissed him. Carlos kissed her, pulling her closer with one arm, the cellophane around the roses crunching slightly. Her middle warmed as she kissed him, and she felt aglow like a burning fire. Carlos kissed her mouth, her cheek, and then hugged her.

"Santa must have brought you what you wanted," he murmured.

Anika stepped back and wagged a finger at him. "Careful, he's already adjusting the naughty and nice list for next year."

Carlos chuckled. His eyes flitted over to the large wrapped gift sitting against the wall. Megan danced around. "Can I open it now? Carlos, can I open it?"

"Yes, I can't wait to see it." He leaned toward Anika and whispered in her ear, "Thanks for waiting for me."

Megan squealed in delight when she pulled off the wrapping paper. "A doll house for me!" She kneeled down and looked at the tiny pieces of furniture and the different colored rooms. Then she jumped into Carlos's arms and hugged him. "I love you!"

"I love you, too, Megan. I'm so glad you like it." Carlos patted her back and he winked at Anika.

Carlos stood and handed Anika a small wrapped gift. "This is for you."

Anika took the gift, running a hand over the silver and green paper. "Thank you."

"Well, that was easy. You're thanking me before you even see what's in it." Carlos laughed when Anika wrinkled her nose at him. She loved how comfortable she felt with him and how everything in the world seemed brighter since he came into her life. The paper crinkled as she tore open the gift, revealing a hand-carved Christmas tree-shaped ornament. The dark cherry wood was carved with several layers of evergreen boughs. A red ribbon was attached to a hook at the top. "This is beautiful!" Anika hung the ornament on her tree and reached out her hand to squeeze Carlos's.

He touched the ornament gently swaying on its red ribbon. "Did you know that the Hope tree wasn't damaged in the fire?"

Anika's eyes widened. "It wasn't?"

Carlos shook his head. "The fire, smoke, and water damage went right up to that point and veered around it. Some people said it was a miracle, and I wondered, why was it a miracle that a fake Christmas tree didn't burn when the new shelves I built in the children's department did? But then I thought of you that first night we met under the Christmas tree." Carlos smiled and pulled Anika closer.

She glanced back at the wooden ornament before turning to face him. "That tree changed my life."

Carlos nodded and held her close. Megan was busy introducing her dolls to their new house, her eyes shining with happiness. Anika felt as if her chest would burst with so much emotion. Love pulsed from every pore, filling up the room. Anika handed Carlos a card. "I'm sorry that it isn't more."

Carlos squeezed her hand, pulling her onto his lap on the couch. "You're the only thing I asked for." He nuzzled her cheek, and then directed his attention to opening the card. Anika could see the words she'd written in black ink against the cream-colored Christmas card from Kenworth's.

Carlos,

 Thanks for saving me and bringing Christmas back to life. Will you help me decorate my Christmas tree again next year?
 I love your heart. Every hopeful beat. You.
 Love,
 Anika

Carlos turned to her and smiled. "Yes, but I wondered if you'd help me decorate a tree at my house? I'm hoping that there will be more people to celebrate there next year."

He touched her cheek and kissed her gently, pulling back to look into her eyes. Anika smiled and leaned forward until her lips met his again. She kissed him until her heart thrummed happily in her chest. And with the sounds of Megan playing around the Christmas tree, Carlos's arms around her, and love in her heart, something happened. It felt like her heart burst from its protective shell.

Anika cried, and she didn't try to stop the tears. She decided that it was okay to cry for the happiness and goodness she saw in Megan's eyes, and Carlos. God loved her, and He sent her someone at Christmas— the time of the Savior's birth to open her eyes and give her hope for Christmas.

Keep reading for a sneak peek of the next book in the Echo Ridge Romance series: **The Kiss Thief**

Carlos's White Chicken Chili
w/Optional Slow-Cooker tips

Ingredients:

1 pound boneless skinless chicken breasts, chopped

1 medium onion, chopped

1 tablespoon olive oil, or use infused flavored olive oil with garlic

2 garlic cloves, crushed

2 cans (14 ounces each) chicken broth or substitute with 28 ounces of water and 2 chicken bouillon cubes

1 can (4 ounces) chopped green chilies

2 teaspoons ground cumin

2 teaspoons dried oregano

1-1/2 teaspoons cayenne pepper

3 cans (14-1/2 ounces each) great northern beans, drained, divided

1 cup (4 ounces) shredded Monterey Jack cheese

Chopped jalapeno pepper, optional

Over medium heat, cook chicken and onion in oil until lightly browned. Add garlic; cook 1 minute longer. Stir in the broth, chilies, cumin, oregano and cayenne; bring to a boil.

For slow-cooker method, sauté onion in olive oil with garlic and then add raw chicken breasts and all other ingredients to crockpot. Cook on low for 8 hours or cook on high for 3-4 hours until chicken is done. Shred chicken right in the crockpot or remove it and dice it to your desired size. Enjoy the chili!

10 servings (2-1/2 quarts).

THE MAPLE LEAVES SKITTERED across the sidewalk and crunched under Britta Klein's black low-heeled shoes as she walked toward the Echo Ridge Library. She paused for a moment to watch a dark red leaf twirl in the slight wind coming from Parley's Canyon. She narrowed her eyes—that leaf was carefree, no expectations, nothing to do but dance with the wind. She huffed. If only her life could be that simple.

It was never wise to give in to dramatics, but Britta had just gotten off the phone after talking to her mother for forty-five minutes and the message was loud and clear: *Find a German man and marry him so I can have some enkelkinder.* Her mother wanted grandchildren so she could spoil them with strudels and kuchen.

Britta put her hand on the cool metal handle of the door to the library, grounding herself before she headed inside to greet the staff of her library. She reminded herself, again, how good it felt to be in charge of the Echo Ridge Library. At the young age of thirty-one, Britta had achieved her dream of becoming head librarian, but the dream carried more stress than she'd ever imagined.

Tomorrow was the kickoff to the huge library fundraiser that Britta had been working on for the past three months. The children's section was in desperate need of capital, and she worried if this venue was not a success, they'd lose patrons. The library board meeting started in fifteen minutes and Britta hoped that all of the key players for the Harvest Hurrah would show up.

The familiar, dry smell of books greeted Britta when she stepped inside. She never tired of that smell—the tart aroma of new books, freshly marked for distribution in Echo Ridge, mixed with the musty scent of books over a hundred years old that patrons could still check out. The library was once a large stone church house built in the mid-1800s. When Britta first moved to Echo Ridge for her entry-level job at the library, she'd fallen in love with the romantic building. A single staircase curved up to a loft that overlooked the open building with its stacks of books. The old choir room adjacent to the loft was now an office and an open room with a couch and table. That's where the board meeting would be held, but when they didn't have meetings, people could sit on the comfortable couch and read with thousands of volumes below them, seemingly waiting for their turn to be picked next.

The rickety lift that lowered into the basement had always captured her imagination—whispering of stolen kisses, shadowed mysteries, and a hideaway to read dime-store novels. Or maybe Britta infused her daydreams onto the ancient elevator. But either way, the lift needed an update so they could move the children's section to the basement. That was of utmost importance according to Marian Montgomery, the assistant librarian and grand-mother, protector, and overlord of all books. The woman was obsessed with order and decimal systems, but in a different way than Britta.

"Shh," Marian shushed a child who jumped up and down with a picture book in front of his frazzled mother.

"Good morning." Britta forced a smile, hoping to soften the tension humming around Marian. Her flat brown hair interlaced with gray was punctuated by the dark glasses hiding the wrinkles around her eyes. Her shoulders turned slightly inward, probably from carrying stacks of bestsellers around the library for the past seven-teen years.

"Noisy ones today. No one can seem to keep their children quiet," Marian grumbled.

"By the end of the month, we'll be able to order the white noise transmitters to cover some of the sound," Britta replied. The state-of-the-art speakers would sit atop each stack of books and transmit a frequency to eliminate some of the noise in the library. The high ceilings of the old church were beautiful with stained-glass windows set in the arches and over the front door, but that feature didn't transfer well when the church became the new library. The extra space contributed to the noise problem. The echoes of children's laughter and whispers carried upwards and echoed right back down. Britta loved the sound, but it drove Marian crazy.

"Well, I'm worried we won't have enough funds for everything we need to do with this old building, so I've come up with an idea to help with the book drive," Marian replied.

Britta brought her view back to ground level. "Oh? What do you have in mind?"

"Oh, no." Marian wagged her finger. "You'll have to wait just like everyone else for the unveiling." She hugged her clipboard closer to her chest.

Hopefully her plans wouldn't involve boxing up patrons under the age of ten and shipping them to Timbuktu.

"I'm heading upstairs to prep for the meeting. I'll talk to you later." Britta waved at Marian and meandered through the stacks to the back of the library.

Britta let her hand trail along the dark walnut railing as she climbed the staircase. The tops of the stacks looked a bit dusty. She made a mental note to have Trish clean them before the weekend. Britta's stomach clenched with nerves when she thought of the prestigious Armand D. Beaumont flying in from France to do a special author reading for Echo Ridge. He had written over fifteen books and was a New York Times bestselling author with quite a following of readers eager to devour his next novel.

When Shennedy Layton had come to her with the idea of bringing in a famous author to kick off the library fundraiser, Britta had immediately thought of Armand because he was related—sort of. Her uncle's sister-in-law had pulled the family strings to get Armand to come to the States.

Britta paused at the oak door which opened into the offices off the old choir loft and turned back to view her beloved library. The framed portrait of the wealthy Vannakin family hung over the circulation desk, reminding everyone of the incredible generosity that had made the Echo Ridge Library possible.

She turned and entered the meeting room, letting the door shut behind her. Britta had only a few moments to prepare before she heard the door creak open.

A blond-haired beauty in her mid-forties popped inside. "I can't believe he's really coming. Britta, it's happening for Echo Ridge!" Shennedy always arrived early and her enthusiasm was catching as she flitted about the room.

"I just hope that Armand will be enough to get this fundraiser into motion. We have a lot of work to do." Britta found herself smiling despite her worries. With

Shennedy there to help her, the Harvest Hurrah would surely be a success. She had done wonders with the Big Barn Boutique, partnering with Kenworth's to create a unique offering of antiques and handmade items. The young woman had plenty of fire and grit, and Britta reminded herself that she could relax and allow her and other board members to relieve some of the stress from her shoulders.

Britta nodded at Kirke Staples, who entered the room inconspicuously and sat down. He was a playwright, but didn't like to talk about it much—at least the one time Britta had tried to get him to come out of his shell. He kept his head down and scrawled out notes on a pad of paper. Hopefully he would contribute to the meeting today.

The owner of Fay's Café, Fay Griffith, came in at the same time as a husband and wife team. They sat near the front, eager to help their beloved library. When the lovely white-haired Mrs. Tumnus arrived, Britta felt reassured once again that the fundraising events were in good hands. The older woman was tiny, maybe only five-foot-three, but she carried a presence that inspired others to do their best.

At five past ten there were seven board members present, and Chayton Liechty slipped in right before Britta called the meeting to order. As a high school teacher and lacrosse coach at Echo Ridge High, his insight had proved valuable to integrate students' needs into the library.

"Thank you all for coming today. We have several things to go over, so I printed these agendas." Britta passed the papers around the table. "First, the book drive kicks off tomorrow. Our goal is to bring in five thousand books. Many of those books will be sold to our patrons through our revolving bookstore so that we can purchase new releases."

"Do you have the manpower to sort through five thousand books?" Fay asked.

"We have all year to get through them," Britta answered. "We store the extra boxes in the basement and put new ones out each month. I've made a request from the city for another part-time librarian who might help with that, but they're waiting to see how the fundraiser goes because the lift project is not optional."

Kirke nodded. "That thing is way past due for an update."

"We also have the white noise speakers, moving the children's section downstairs, purchasing new stacks to fill the space that creates ..." Britta held up her fingers as she ticked off each item. "... a new computer table, and furniture for the children's section."

"Wow, this will be like a whole new library once you're finished," Shennedy said.

Britta beamed. "That's the plan."

"How much do we need to earn from the fundraiser to cover all of these projects?" Chayton asked.

Britta knew the amount, $23,583.07, to the penny. But she was hesitant to voice the total. It sounded outrageous. She swallowed, looking at the expectant faces of the library board; then she smiled. "This year we have a lot more going for us than the community has seen. My goal is to reach $25,000 with all projects combined."

Shennedy clapped her hands, but Kirke's mouth dropped open. Shennedy patted him on the arm. "Don't worry. With Armand coming, it'll blow our celebration through the roof. People are going to be driving in from all over New York to see him."

The board members continued to discuss how they could meet their goals and several of them seemed worried about the amount needed. Ideas were shared about cutting back in order to get the most vital things the library needed. A healthy debate ensued with each person noting how valid all of the items on Britta's list were and the dilemma they faced.

Britta didn't let the scary amount of money derail the meeting. She continued on in the next breath. "In the meantime, if you could take ten posters each and place them around town, I'd appreciate it. These have all the dates and info about our fundraiser, Armand's visit, and the Harvest Hurrah." She passed out a sheaf of glossy posters to each board member.

"Good work, Britta," Chayton said. "I'll post some of these at the high school."

"Thank you for your help. The city of Echo Ridge is depending on us to meet our goals, so no pressure." She smiled. "I'll see you next week."

Continue reading the next book in the Echo Ridge Romance series: **The Kiss Thief,** *available in ebook, print, and audio. For more information visit*

www.rachellechristensen.com

*This heart-warming, inspirational romance from award-winning and bestselling author Rachelle J. Christensen is part of the Echo Ridge Romance Collection.

Although you can read the books as standalones, you don't want to miss this exciting series:

Hope for Christmas

The Kiss Thief

The Princess Bride of Riodan

Coming Home to Love

Her Guy Next Door Fake Fiancé

Photo by Erin Summerill

Rachelle writes mystery/suspense, clean romance, and women's fiction. She is the mother of a large family and she solves the case of the missing shoe on a daily basis. She enjoys raising chickens, laughing with her family, and traveling with her husband. She graduated cum laude from Utah State University with a degree in psychology and a minor in music.

Rachelle is the award-winning author of over twenty books, including *The Soldier's Bride (a Kindle Scout Selection)*, the Rone award winner for mystery, *River Whispers, Diamond Rings Are Deadly Things, Hawaiian Masquerade,* and *the Echo Ridge Romance series*. Her novella, "Silver Cascade Secrets," was included in the Rone Award–winning *Timeless Romance Anthology, Fall Collection*.

Join Rachelle's VIP mailing list to learn more about upcoming books and get your free book at www.rachellechristensen.com.

Free Book!

Thrills for the Heart

FOR A LIMITED TIME

Sign up for Rachelle's
VIP Mailing List
to get your *FREE* book.

★ ★ ★ ★ ★

Get started here:
www.rachellechristensen.com